NIXON

JANE ACE

Playlist

Cher Lloyd-Baddest
Lana Del Rey – Gods & Monsters
Ruelle – Monsters
Meg Myers – Jealous Sea
Raphael Lake, Aaron Levy, Daniel Ryan Murphy – Prisoner
Valerie Broussard – A Little Wicked
Two Feet – I Feel Like I'm Drowning
Bring me the horizon – Can you feel my heart
Bring me the horizon – Throne
Chase Atlantic - Church
Chase and status – Let you go
Dutch Melrose – RUNRUNRUN
Sofia Isella – Hot Gum
Breaking Benjamin – Dance With The Devil
ZAYN, Taylor Swift – I Don't Wanna Live Forever
Rezz ft Dove Cameron – Taste of You

"If I am an angel,
paint me with black wings."

~Anne Rice (The Vampire Armand)

One

Nixon

There is nothing that kills a hard on quicker than a call from your dying father.

Alexander Lennox always did have an impeccable talent for ruining my happiness by any means possible. It didn't matter what it was, from horse riding as a child to boozing with my mates as a teen. If it brought me joy, then my father would find a way to put a stop to it.

I guess even on his deathbed, old habits die hard.

Some might say it is a little too soon for jokes, but fuck the old sod.

I admit that I have been waiting *not* so patiently for this day to come.

I have been summoned back home to the family estate, where he wants to give me his last demands, I'm sure, instead I will be going to ensure that he has indeed taken his last breath.

I guess it is a good thing the flight from London to the Scottish Highlands is only a few hours; I wouldn't want to miss out on his grand finale. My father's assistant and personal nurse have been trying to get me to come to his beside for a few weeks now, however I have been sending them to voicemail, intent on leaving it until the last possible minute to return home.

It looks like that minute has finally arrived.

Hopefully, the 12-year-old Macallan is still in the cellar. I plan on toasting my good fortune.

Turning back towards my bed and the woman lying in it, sprawled as naked as the day she was born, blonde locks a scattered mess across the pillows, I curse my father internally once again.

Tonight would have been fun.

"Sorry, gorgeous." I aim a playful smirk at her to soften the blow of my next words. "I am going to need to take a rain check. I have some urgent business that I, unfortunately, cannot ignore."

Propping herself on her elbows, her glorious full breasts bounce with the motion of her flicking her hair to one side so her pout is in full view.

"Seriously, Nixon?" She spreads her legs wide, giving me a full view of her glistening centre. Unfortunately, her voice takes on a high-pitched whine that would have killed my erection if my father hadn't already done the honours.

Groaning, I run a hand through my dark hair. Getting rid of her is going to be harder than I thought.

"Please put your clothes back on, Sophia. Do not make me ask again." I grab my abandoned black tee from the floor and pull it back on. "Next time, I won't be so pleasant about it."

With the grace of the prima ballerina that she is, she slides her supple limbs off the bed and gathers her dress and panties, huffing the whole way to my en suite. "God, you really are an asshole. I should have listened to my sister."

I give her a dark and condescending chuckle.

Yes, you should have.

I fucked her sister a few months ago. Yes, she knew about it, and yes, she was still eager to get me between the sheets.

"Careful, Sophia, you know if I call you when I am done, you will come running." I talk loud enough that she will hear me through the bathroom door, and I am already setting about packing a bag.

I pack light, having no intention of staying longer than necessary. I will be back on the return flight before his body is cold.

The door swings open and Sophia struts out, looking as put together as before. Her bony hand slides down my back over the black material. "So, you are going to call me when you are done?"

The pouty, spoiled princess act is gone, and the seductress is back in full. Girls like Sophia are used to getting their own way. Me and my cock are in her sights now and she will do anything to have me, even sacrifice her pride.

There is no bigger turn off.

"Not in this lifetime, gorgeous. Now, if you follow me out, I will have my driver drop you home."

Unsurprisingly, like a lost little sheep, she follows at my heels. Maybe for once in his life, my father has done me a favour.

***

The sun is rising as the Lennox family private jet lands at Inverness Airport four hours after my father's call. A Land Rover waits on the tarmac at my request, and the driver jumps out as I throw my bag in the backseat.

"The roads look clear, sir. You should make good time back home." The young guy, who looks vaguely familiar, throws me the key fob and climbs into an identical vehicle behind my own.

Home.

Lennox House has never been my home. My father made sure of that. At thirteen, I was shipped off to boarding school. Eton College couldn't have felt further from everything I ever knew. Nothing but the best for Alexander Lennox, and his sole heir, was acceptable. So, he sent me to the place that educated the crème de la crème of society. The spawns of royalty and world leaders, all crammed into one location. A breeding ground for nepotism and entitlement. Not that I was much different, as I am the heir to the Lennox titles and lands upon my father's death. So, it was easy to fit in amongst my peers, and they soon became my family.

As the years passed by, I stopped going home for winter break. Choosing to spend time at my best friend's family estate in the lake district instead. His father was the deputy prime minister at the time, so Alexander happily encouraged potential relationships which could benefit our family in the future. However, the people I eventually went into business with are a little less savoury than the politicians and owners of Fortune 500s, and that is saying something.

From Eton, I attended Oxford University and I have barely spent much time in Scotland since. So little, in fact, that disguising my accent is now delightfully easy. I find that it helps minimise the personal questions. For some reason, people hear a Scottish accent and they want to know all about where you are from. Which is a memory that I actively try to erase.

The sky is surprisingly clear for late November. The air so fresh and crisp I can't resist the urge to roll down the windows despite the chill. There really is nothing like the clear air up here, and my lungs delight in the fresh oxygen, having gotten used to the polluted city as my hair whips against my face and the frozen wind nips at my nose and cheeks.

I can't help the smile that tugs at my lips, thinking of my mates back in London. They would need full fleece-lined coats and gloves and call me a madman for sitting here in nothing more than a hoodie and relishing the sharp bite from the icy gusts.

As I get closer to the estate, the roads get smaller and more curved, and despite the years that have passed, I still know the route like the back of my hand. I travel deeper into the imposing mountains with the high peaks hidden in the fog and the waterfalls partly frozen on their descent through the rocky face of the hills. The wild and rugged landscape flies past in an array of vivid greens and deep yellows, nature being unmistakably in winter's grasp. The untouched terrain feels alive and threatens danger if you wonder off the beaten track or dare to stay out past sundown.

I guess that is one of the things that never left me. The natural hostility and hardness ingrained into my very being from being born into an environment such as this one.

Wondering if I will miss my home country, I take in my surroundings and soak it all in for one of the last times. I guess I will have no need to return after this visit.

The Rover carries me down the uneven single-track road with ease. I am now officially on the Lennox estate, although I am still a mile or two away from the main house. Stags graze in the otherwise silent woods, only looking up at the soft purr of the engine. They are, no doubt, used vehicles coming in and out at the west side of the grounds. If I remember correctly, the groundsmen prefer any hunting parties to stay clear of the main driveway, so they will know they are safe in these parts. Through a break in the trees, a thick turret stands proudly above the tree line. The dark grey slate a striking contrast to the luscious green pines.

The Lennox estate is one of the last few privately owned stately homes in the country that is not open to the public and still occupied by the original family descendants. One of the few things my mother and father agreed upon when she was still alive was that Lennox House should be kept as a private estate at all costs for as long as there is still a legitimate bloodline.

At twenty-five, with no intention of settling down any time soon, or at all, Alexander Lennox will not live to see if his bloodline will continue, and the thought of the pain that must cause him thrills me.

I clear the tree lined entryway, and the wide circular double driveway with a large fountain depicting Atlas carrying the world on his back comes into immediate view. The house itself stands unchanged and exactly how I remember it.

Firstly, I never understood why it was named Lennox House instead of Lennox Castle. With its grand towers and gothic turrets, 'Lennox House' is most definitely a castle. Its imposing presence is a stark contrast to the glorious wilderness of its surroundings, and there are more rooms than any normal person would know what to do with. Palatial gardens fall to the back of the property and in the forest to the east lays the ruins of a 15th century chapel.

And as the 16th Earl of Lennoxshire in waiting, I am soon to inherit it all, and if I have my way, I will be the last Lennox Earl.

My ancestors will be turning in their graves.

I kill the engine and sit in silence, taking a moment to compose my thoughts before heading inside.

I am the man my father made me. As far as he is aware, I am cold, heartless and ruthless in business. What he doesn't realise is that it doesn't end there for me. I have no compassion, sympathy or empathy except for a carefully selected chosen few in my life. I don't need more than one hand to count the people in life who I trust, and not one person on the list bears the name Lennox.

Deciding not to waste any more time, I push from the car. Knowing how much the blatant sign of disrespect will irk him, I don't bother to change, and head straight to my father's suite, wearing my casual jeans and hoodie.

I stride through the darkened hallways. It is like even the house itself is holding its breath for the inevitable, my long steps eating up the distance in no time. Pushing the door open, I don't bother with knocking. This place will be mine in a matter of hours, and I want my father to see the evidence of that before he goes.

There, in the middle of the four-poster bed fit for a medieval king, lies Alexander Lennox, the 15th Earl of Lennoxshire. I could tell by the strain in his voice when we spoke last night, that it must have taken the last of his energy to call me. But this is even better than I imagined.

My father was a believer in 'spare the rod, spare the child' and the walls of this house have heard my cries and begging plenty of times before I was shipped off for someone else to raise.

Alexander was always an imposing man, and I take after him in many ways. My sharp features, raven hair, and dark eyes to match are passed down through the Lennox genes. Feared by the men and worshipped by the women, my father was adored and respected by everyone but me, it would seem. Looking at him now, he is a shell of himself, hooked up to painkillers through and IV, and an oxygen mask covering most of his frail face.

A sinister smile pulls at my mouth as I slowly approach his beside.

Karma.

I clear my throat loudly, purposefully disturbing his peaceful state, and tuck my hands into my front pockets.

I consider pulling my phone out and scrolling through mindless content to highlight how little I am affected by his suffering, but I don't want to miss a single moment of what is happening here.

There are many ways we are similar, yes. However, there is one definitive way we are drastically different. For all the ways I am a bastard, I would never raise my hands to a child or to a woman.

Anyone who beats a helpless child, in my opinion, deserves to die a long and painful death.

Unfortunately for Alexander Lennox, he thought that his money and power put him above the repercussions of the universe.

It did not.

As his dark brown eyes meet my own, relief flashes through them before they flare in anger.

"I am sorry that I am late, Father, but there were one hundred other things I would rather be doing." I lean over him and brush his hair away from his face. "You look like shit, by the way. Don't listen to what anyone else tells you. They lie because you pay them."

Straightening to my full height, I tilt my head and chuckle. "Well, not for long, as it will be me that they tell their lies to soon. In a few hours, by the look of you, you won't make it to midnight."

I kneel at my father's side, and to anyone watching, I must look like a doting son grieving the ill health of his most beloved father. I slide my hand over his cold, frail one and bring my mouth close to his ear.

Speaking slowly, so he doesn't miss a word, I continue. "I am going to sell it, Father. I am going to strip this estate down to the bones and sell it for parts. I am going to sell Lennox House to the National Trust and let them build a fucking adventure playground in the gardens and lastly the only children I will ever sire will be bastards. No more Lennox House, no more Earls of Lennoxshire. Your legacy. Ends. Here."

As I knew it would, my father's breathing becomes even more laboured than before, and the machine monitoring his heart starts beeping frantically, triggering the alarm. With the last of his energy, he tries to grab me with the hand I am holding, hands that inflicted years of pain and suffering to his only child, but I keep my grip on him tight, showing one last display of strength as I twist my head away from the doorway, where I expect a nurse to charge through any second and give him my most devilishly triumphant smile.

"My, how the tables have turned, Father. Checkmate." His eyes widen, and the beeping stops and turns into one long, consistent drone.

It's done.

I drop his lifeless hand and make my way to the door in search of that Macallan.

The weight I have been carrying for years lifts more with every step that takes me further from his body.

Two

Nixon

The mahogany door swings open as I reach for the handle, and body hurtles straight into me. Grabbing the person by the shoulders, I look down in confusion, my view of the intruder blocked by a mane of red hair.

The woman freezes in my hands, her body turning rigid as I push her back and hold her at an arm's length. Wanting to get a full view of whoever feels comfortable enough to storm into this room uninvited. Perhaps she is the nurse who has been such a nuisance these past few months.

"Who the hell are you?"

She is a small, delicate thing, and she flutters in my hold, trying to break free like a little wild robin who has flown into a cage.

"I will not ask you again." I squeeze my hands tighter, letting her know this is her final warning.

With the desperation she is trying to break free of my hold, my suspicions are quickly growing.

My eyes drop to her bare feet—not an intruder, then.

Tipping her head, her blue eyes scan my face before nervously dropping to my chest.

"I am Karina, sir. Your father's nurse." Her voice is husky yet melodic. She is Scottish, but her intonations tell me that she isn't from around these parts.

I drop my hands from her shoulders and tip her chin with my thumb and forefinger. Narrowing my eyes at her, I ask, "Nurse?"

"Please, sir, I must check on him." I drop my hand from her face in annoyance. Her persistence with my father is frustrating, to say the least.

"He is gone. Tell me, why did you not come sooner?" I sneer at her accusingly, as if there is anything that she could have done to save him, and as if I actually care.

"It was his last wish to talk with you and he insisted on privacy when you arrived. Also, your father had signed a DNR. He would not have wanted anyone to interfere."

"A DNR?" I am confident I know the meaning, but I just want her to confirm.

"A 'Do not resuscitate,' sir." Sliding out of my way, she pads gracefully towards the bed before checking my father's vitals.

Karina turns off the machine, which still rings through the room, and unhooks all the wires before gently pulling his white bedsheet over his body.

I frown as she makes the sign of the cross over her chest and whispers a Gaelic prayer I don't understand.

Alexander Lennox doesn't deserve a blessing of any kind, especially from a creature as exquisite as her. God knows he won't have a free pass through the pearly gates, so her efforts on his behalf are useless.

Something isn't sitting right. My father always prized professionalism over everything else. This young woman is claiming she is his nurse, yet here she is, not even wearing shoes, never mind a uniform. Karina is beautiful. Anyone who spares her a glance would notice, and young, much too young, in fact, to be a fully qualified nurse.

The hairs on the back of my neck prickle.

"Were you fucking him?" I spit the first words and most likely explanation that comes to my mind. For some inexplicable reason, the thought disgusts me, but I couldn't blame my father. Karina is absolutely stunning. With the air of a wild, untameable thoroughbred, that would be enough to temp any hot-blooded male.

Her steps falter as she rounds the bed, tucking in the sheets. "Excuse me?" Her long red tresses swing over her shoulder, kissing her waist.

"I am not in the habit of repeating myself, Miss...?" I raise a brow in expectation.

"Campbell." Karina balls her tiny little fists at her sides in a pathetic attempt at concealing her frustrations. Her cheeks blush an enticing shade of pink, and I surprisingly find myself wondering if her body would flush the same colour if I were to tease and suck on her perky little tits.

"Miss Campbell, however, considering the circumstances, I will make an allowance." I drop my chin, looking up at her through my lashes as I take slow, deliberate steps in her direction. "Were you having sex with him?"

"No, I was not." Her eyes flare, and her fury warms my blood. "I was his nurse. Your father was receiving end-of-life care, Mr Lennox. He was in no state for such activities. He couldn't even bathe himself."

"So, you were sucking his cock, then?" I scoff at her, like the answer is obvious. Giving her my back like she is a full-grown conclusion when, in actual fact, I need to distract myself before I get a semi from verbally sparring with this captivating beauty.

By her reaction, I believe that her relationship with my father was platonic, but there is something about this little redhead and getting under her skin in the most fun I have had in months.

"Don't you dare!" Her voice shakes with anger, and I smother the smile that threatens my lips before turning and giving her my signature blank stare. "Don't you dare make assumptions about me and slight my character when you know nothing about me."

"Oh, but, my dear Karina, I am afraid I *can dare* to do whatever I wish." Invading her personal space, I step up to her getting as close as possible without touching her, and dip my head, speaking into the crown of her fiery hair. "This is now *my* house, *my* land, *my* titles. You now answer to *me*. I. Own. You.

A soft growl erupts from the back of her throat, and despite everything, it kicks my heart in to gear. I can feel my blood heating further. This will not do.

"That wasn't a no, Karina. Not that it matters anyway. You are no longer needed at Lennox House. Pack your bags. I am feeling generous, so I will give you twenty-four hours to organise yourself." I leave the room, knowing that she will follow me.

Despite the distraction that Karina has momentarily provided, I can't stand to be in a room for one second longer with my poisonous father and his now rotting corpse. His presence is ruining my good mood.

"I am afraid I won't be doing that, Mr Lennox." As expected, the sound of her bare feet padding behind me fills the hallways as she stomps after me.

"I am afraid that you will be. You will receive any outstanding wages owed to you within the week." I need her out of here as soon as possible. She will be a distraction, a roadblock in my plans. I am not sure how, but I can smell the trouble on her a mile away.

"No, you are missing the point. I have a contract."

"Not a contract with me." What does this woman not understand about anything I have just threatened?

"A contract with the Lennox estate. It states that after the passing of the earl, I have thirty days to look for other employment."

I stop on the stairs leading down to the foyer. She is three stairs above me and only just meets my eyeline. "You're lying. My father would never agree to something like that."

I say the last part more to myself than to her.

"Well, perhaps you didn't know your father as well as you thought that you did." If I am not mistaken, her words are meant as a challenge.

This chick really thinks she has the moral high ground with me?

Like I said, trouble.

Ascending the three steps and closing the space between us, I narrow my gaze, pinning her in place through her glacial eyes. Such a magnificent contrast to the warmth of her hair.

My hands twitch at my sides as I resist the urge to wrap her hair around my fist. I wonder if she is this defiant when she is lying on her back? "Send me a copy of this contract immediately," is all I manage to push past my lips, in a poor attempt at pushing my inappropriate thoughts to the back of my mind.

Fucking the staff would be very tragically Downton Abbey of me.

"You won't find any clauses, Mr Lennox. It is an iron-clad contract. Your father made sure of it."

That bastard! He has done this to fuck with me.

But for what reason, and why would he care so much about his nurse?

Maybe she really was sucking him off?

Again, and for reasons unbeknown to me, the thought makes me want to vomit. Not the act itself, or the fact that it may have involved my father, but the fact that it may have involved the little vixen standing before me. With her arms crossed and her head high, like she has a right to make demands in my fucking house.

***

The cellar at Lennox House has an adjacent cigar lounge. A place I know my father liked to spend a lot of time. So, it only seems fitting that I toast his departure in here, drinking his most expensive bottles while flicking ash onto his favourite Persian rug.

Sipping on my whisky, I scroll through the copy of Karina's contract I demanded my father's assistant to email to me.

"...Upon the death of the patient (Mr Alexander Lennox), the employee (Miss Karina Campbell) will be given the grace of 30 days to vacate the Property (Lennox House, Lennoxshire, Inverness shire, Scotland). If Miss Campbell is dismissed before the death of the patient, or evicted before the 30-day grace period is complete, a sum of £50 000 000 will be awarded..."

What in the hell was my father playing at?

There must be more to this than my father doing something out of the kindness of his heart. In my twenty-five years on this earth, I'd never seen my father pull a stunt so selfless.

I just don't get it; Karina being his lover seemed like the most logical explanation.

A thought comes to me, and I am making the call without checking what time of the day it is. My father's lawyers will answer my calls no matter the day or time.

"Nixon," Gerrard, my father's most trusted attorney, answers on the second ring. "I am so sorry to hear the news. Please accept my condolences."

"Was he of sound mind?" I demand, forgoing the pleasantries.

"Excuse me?"

"You heard me. Was the old bastard of sound mind, or had the cancer eaten his brain? He has made an unwise business deal, and I want to know if it stands." Throwing back the last of the Macallan, I waste no time in pouring myself a double.

"Ah," the prick almost laughs, "if you are referring to the employment of Miss Campbell, then yes, your father was of sound mind. In fact, he knew you would question it, and I was given strict instructions to inform you that it is quite soundproof."

Rubbing the palm of my hand into my eye to ease the impending migraine I can feel creeping up on me, I try to keep my shit together, but it is useless. I kill the call and hurl the crystal tumbler across the room. It smashes against the hunter green wall and scatters across the mahogany floor.

My plans to sell Lennox House and surrounding lands will have to wait 30 days. Which, with a quick calculation, will take us into the Christmas holiday, so it will need to wait until after the new year. Everything closes at Hogmanay up here and the few days that follow.

Fifty million pounds, that would be a sizable chunk out of the sale.

Looks like I am not flying home as soon as I intended.

Because, of course, I can't leave a stranger unattended in my ancestral home. Over the holidays, to do whatever it is she has been doing since she got here.

I have 30 days to find out the hold this little minx had over my father.

Three

Karina

Nixon Lennox is everything I worried he would be.

Cold, unfeeling, unapproachable.

Heartless.

The things he said to his own flesh and blood when he was taking his last breaths will stay with me forever. What kind of son would taunt his father in such a disgusting manner? The earl was on his deathbed, yes. However, I am certain it was Nixon and his confessions that pushed him over the edge.

Nixon's cruelty, I was expecting. What I did not expect is how breathtaking his beauty would be. Any pictures around the house are of a young boy who looks to be on the brink of being a teenager. Long, awkward limbs, and black hair that falls over his ghostly pale face, purposefully hiding him from the lens and the world around him.

Not now, now he stands proudly, his frame well over 6 feet and no longer gangly and awkward, but controlled and sculpted to perfection. He must spend all his days in the gym working out. Nixon's raven locks are swept off his face, putting his sharp features on full display, making him almost uncomfortable to look at head on.

It was nearly intolerable to look directly into his eyes when he demanded to know me. I am used to being around intimidating men, yet there is something alluring about Nixon's dangerous presence. The air around him is charged with something electric that commands your full attention if you dare to look into the eye of the storm, but one quick reminder of how disgusting he was to his father in his time of need, is enough to erase any interest in his sinful beauty from my eyes, leaving nothing but the rot that is hidden beneath.

Nixon lives in London, so I am hopeful he will return as soon as the situation allows. I can't imagine having to live in the same property as him for the next month, no matter how vast this estate is. And frankly, I will have no choice. I have nowhere else to go, unless I want to sleep on the streets.

There is nothing out there for me, no safe or loving home for me to return to.

Alexander knew that, hence the clause in my contract. He also knew his son would have a problem with it. Which is why I immediately informed him that his efforts would be wasted if he tried to break the contract.

Lennox House is one of the safest places I can be right now. Hidden out of sight and off the radar.

Alexander had an affair with my mother before her untimely death many years ago. He was recently a widower himself, and he would always bring me gifts when he came to visit my mother.

Unfortunately, after their relationship ended and my mother's death, monsters from her past managed to catch up with me. So, I fled to the first person I could think of with enough power to keep me untraceable. The thing is, I am not a fully qualified nurse. I have only completed my first two years, yet Alexander told me to keep that to myself, and as far as anyone was concerned, I was his new full-time, live-in nurse.

Mr Lennox didn't want treatment. He didn't want to be cured. He merely requested I keep him pain free and as comfortable as possible.

I guess he saw it as a final act of gratitude towards my mother for bringing him comfort in a time of great sorrow.

So, to hear his own flesh and blood curse him, when he had shown me nothing but great kindness, is an injustice I will not stand for. Nixon Lennox has another thing coming if he thinks that I will just stand back and watch him walk all over me.

I manage to go the rest of the day without a word from Nixon. Keeping myself busy, helping organise funeral arrangements. Honestly, there is not much I can help with, though. For a man of Alexander's status, there are certain protocols that must be followed. So, a little before dinner, I disappear to my room to shower before heading back down to the kitchens to eat with the rest of the house staff. I have been welcomed with open arms by them, and I couldn't have hoped for more.

Ryan, the games keeper for the estate, grew up here and has recently taken over from his retired father. He was raised on this land and knows it like the back of his hand. We both make a beeline for the stew at once, arriving before the pot at the same time.

"I don't think so, you little hellion. Last time, you left none for the rest of us," he teases me and wraps his arms round my waist from behind. "You wouldn't know it by looking at you, but we learned the hard way that you eat like a horse. Seriously, where do you put it all?"

The full table cheers as he swings my body one-eighty, and I can't help the screech of laughter that erupts from my belly.

"Hey! It's not my fault you were late. If you're not fast, you're last."

"Oh, it's like that, is it?" Ryan dips me backwards, and more laughter explodes from me as I brace myself.

Our laughter dies when we realise everyone else in the room has fallen silent. Ryan and I look to them, in wonder, grins still splitting our faces.

It's then I notice Nixon standing in the doorway to the kitchen. Arms folded across his chest and his eyes narrowed in on Ryan's familiar hold around my waist.

Gone are the black jeans and t-shirt, replaced instead with black slacks and a white shirt. Although they are worn just as casually, with his top three buttons undone, showing a silver chain of some sort, and the sleeves rolled to his elbows in an uninformed way.

His dark eyes are as intense as before, and his midnight hair looks like a stylist has spent hours perfecting a sexy bedhead look. When really, he has probably just run his hand through it one too many times.

Unless he has just rolled out of bed with someone... I can't say I'm sure he didn't bring someone with him on this visit.

Does Nixon have a girlfriend?

Unexpected jealousy burns my throat so intensely, the question almost spits itself out onto the floor in front of us all.

Then I remember what he said to his father about heirs and tell myself that Nixon is obviously not the relationship type.

I'm not sure if that makes me feel better or worse.

Nixon doesn't say a word, doesn't even blink. He just stares, his eyes flicking to my face, and then back down to Ryan's hold on me.

Ryan doesn't get the memo, but for reasons I can't explain, my body obeys Nixon's silent demand, and I slip free of Ryan's hold and out of his reach.

He gives a nod so slight, I would have missed it if I wasn't transfixed on his face.

"Miss Campbell, you will be dining with me tonight. We have some things we need to discuss." Nixon leaves me with the view of his muscular back as he walks in the direction of the stairs the lead up to the main house.

Oh, boy. This can't be good.

He disappears, and I turn to the rest of the room, who are all as wide mouthed as me.

Maggie, the house cook, breaks the silence first. "Well, child, off you pop. You mustn't leave our new earl waiting."

Nixon sits at the head of the grand table, a fire roaring in the grate at his back. He truly looks like Satan's heir, not from any lands in this realm.

His skin is pale, making his dark eyes stand out in the warm glow as they track me across the room.

The closer I get to him, I can see the fire's reflection dancing in his pupils, making him look even more sinister than before.

He sips a glass of red wine, never breaking his gaze from mine. I, however, can't help but watch as his throat bobs as he slowly swallows.

That's the thing I've noticed about Nixon. Nothing he does is rushed. Every move he makes seems effortless yet purposeful.

Looking down at myself, I cannot help but feel incredibly underdressed. My black yoga pants and cream knitted jumper, not the usual attire for the formal dining room, I am sure of it.

In all my time here so far, I am yet to step foot into this room.

Dark wooden panels cover the walls, prized stag heads from through the generations adorn the walls, and fresh wildflowers spill out of their vases on the side consoles. A solid wooden table that can seat at least thirty people is bare, besides the place Nixon is seated at, and the setting next to him, which I assume is for me.

Yet the piece that takes my breath away is the grand marble fireplace. The opening so large, I could stand inside if it was not lit.

Nixon watches me like a hawk silently as I take the space in, eyes wide in wonder.

I arrive at his side and reach out a hand to pull my chair, but Nixon beats me to it. He unfolds himself while simultaneously sliding my chair back.

The gentleman bread into his DNA through generations wins out this time around.

Whispering "thank you" as he tucks my chair in, I watch from the corner of my eye as he takes his position at the head of the table on my right, reclining lazily, like a bored king on his throne.

"Wine?" he asks with a sweeping hand in the direction of the red bottle between us. His long fingers are adorned with silver rings that look aged with wear and time.

"Yes, please." I clear the nervous lump in my throat, wondering why I have been asked up here. I know it is not so that Nixon can wine and dine me. "That would be lovely, thank you."

Pouring the red liquid, Nixon watches as it cascades into the large Bordeaux glass, his eyebrows drawn into a frown as he switches and fills his own cup.

Lifting the glass, he swirls it and sniffs the wine, his intense glare fixed on the liquid as he speaks in a low, cold voice that causes the hairs on the back of my neck to stand. "Ryan. Are you and he an item?"

I stand, the sound of the chair scrapping against the floor. I don't know who he thinks he is, but if this is the reason he called me in here then I refuse to stick around and be interrogated about personal matters.

"Sit. Down. Now." His naturally dominant voice leaves no room for negotiation, and I pause mid-air. A few seconds pass before my brain kicks back in from the shock of his command and my body's natural instinct to obey.

"I don't know who you think you are talking to? You may be the king of your castle, but you are not the master of me."

"Sit the fuck down, or I will tie you to the chair," he threatens again in a calm and steady voice. Nixon knows he doesn't have to raise his voice for his threat to be taken seriously.

But that is not what has me frozen on the spot; it is the look in his eyes. Like he is challenging me to disobey him, as though there is nothing he would love more than to chase me down and strap me up against my will.

I must be sick in the head, because my stomach flips at the images my brain is conjuring. It's the stress of being in his presence, it must be. It is exhausting just being in the same room as Nixon.

Deciding to pick and choose my battles, I give up the fight and conserve my energy for the next one. Because there will be a next one. I lower myself back into my chair and reach for my goblet of wine with a shaky hand. Taking a gulp, I consider my words carefully. Unsure why he is asking or, like in a game of chess, how much of the truth I should give him.

"Not exactly."

Dark, penetrating eyes find their way to mine, and he tips his head as if considering how he feels about my answer.

"Not exactly?" he repeats my words and swirls the blood-red liquid. "Interesting."

It is?

Nixon's movements are so smooth and sure, they are almost sensual. The wine circles the glass, and he finally takes a sip.

Fixated, I watch his smooth throat bob as he savours what I can only assume is a very expensive Merlot.

Unease fills me at his calm demeanour. He is like a panther, waiting for the right time to pounce.

"I was under the impression that staff relations were not against the rules." If I don't look directly at him, I can keep my voice strong and resolute.

He nods and sets his glass quietly back on the table. "Yes, that is correct, Miss Campbell. As long as it does not affect your work here. Yet it would seem that your work here is done." I open my mouth to defend myself, but he holds his hand up, silencing me. "I will honour the terms of your contract; however, I will not allow you to distract my staff."

"What are you saying?"

"I am saying," he sneers, baring his teeth slightly, "that whatever it is, exactly, that you and he have going on, it stops here. You are no longer an employee of this estate; therefore, you will not be distracting my staff while you reside here."

"Give me something to do, then."

"Excuse me?" Nixon's voice is deadly calm, but his eyes darken until it is impossible to distinguish between pupil and iris.

"Give me a new job." I push on with my plan, despite Nixon's obvious barely restrained rage.

"Is this so I will allow you two to keep fucking around after hours?" He narrows his eyes accusingly, his expression hard and dispassionate.

I huff at his audacity. Who the hell does he think he is? Although, I cannot say that I am surprised. He did, after all, ask me point-blank if I had been sleeping with his father. "No, it is not. I never planned on freeloading during this time. I just need to figure out my next move. Probably apply for a visa out of the country. I would like to be kept busy while I do that."

His full lips curl with distaste. "A Visa, to where?"

"That really is none of your business, Mr Lennox." I tip my chin up, glaring at him directly. He has pissed me off now. I don't care how nervous he likes to make me. He has continuously crossed the line and he should know I have boundaries.

We sit for a minute, in a staring contest. A battle of wills, and I am determined not to break first. Then, suddenly, like the predator I know he is, Nixon kicks out a muscular leg, hooks his foot around the leg of my chair, and drags me in his direction. In a blink of an eye, I am within his grasp, sitting facing him, with each of his knees encasing mine. Slowly, a wicked smile splits his lips, and my heart drops. I know I am not going to like what he is about to say.

"Very well, Miss Campbell. You will be my personal assistant for the remainder of your time here at Lennox House. On call for my every need." Nixon reaches out one of his ring-adorned hands and tucks a stray strand of hair behind my ear.

My heart beats so wildly in my chest, I am sure that he can hear it. His eyes drop to linger on my parted lips, and to my horror, I think he is going to lean in and capture them with his own. Instead, he dips them to the shell of my ear, his voice a dangerous whisper. "You're not ready for that yet," he taunts, reading my mind. "Oh, and don't worry. I plan on keeping you very busy."

Nixon downs the rest of his drink before pushing away from the table and storming out of the room, our dinner over as he leaves me alone and full of nothing but red wine and dread.

***

There is something about the Scottish Highlands that just hits differently. The sound of nature, the birds, the water, the fresh air, the greens and purples from the Heather-covered hills. It is like you have been transported to a different time, and you don't need a vivid imagination to envisage the history that has taken place in the untouched glens.

A stream runs down the side of the gardens, bracketed by wildflowers and rocks. It continues under an ancient bridge, weak with age and no longer in use, before joining Loch Loni, which the Lennox estate was built on the banks of.

I sit on the stone bridge, my feet dangling over the edge, and watch the early winter sunset. The days are short up here at this time of year. The sun disappears in the late afternoon, meaning there are plenty of fires burning in the house throughout the winter.

It is perfection, and there is no place I would rather be than right here in this moment. I inhale the fresh air of the first day of December, the smell of burning logs floating from nearby.

Since our dinner last night, if you could even call it that, Nixon has left me alone. He is likely compiling a list of all the debasing work he has planned for me. As it is Monday tomorrow, I suspect he will put me to work bright and early.

Dusting off my jeans, I head back in the direction of the house. My breath is visible in the air, and snow has been forecast for the early hours, so it is for the best that I take refuge inside. The late Mr Lennox insisted that my bedroom be near his, in case he needed pain relief throughout the night, and I make a mental note to check if Nixon wants to move me downstairs to the staff quarters.

I slide off my boots, changing into my indoor shoes in the cloakroom, and head upstairs through the cinnamon-scented hallways. It would seem that now we are officially in December, Maggie is wasting no time in getting into the holiday spirit.

Closing my bedroom door, I smile inwardly, seeing that someone has had the fire in my room lit.

Ryan probably did it earlier, as he knows I like to wander outside at this time of day.

The room is dark, beside the orange flames dancing in the grate. The flickering light casts shadows along the walls, and I am drawn in the direction of its source. I hold my hands close, heating my frozen skin and soaking up the soothing sound of the crackling logs.

"I will miss this the most when I move downstairs," I confess aloud to the darkness.

"Who said you are moving downstairs?" I grip on to the stone fireplace, catching my balance. A smooth, deep tone from the other side of the room could only be from one person.

Nixon Lennox sits in the velvet forest-green armchair. His sharp gaze fixes on me, legs spread wide, relaxed like he owns the place.

Well, I guess he does, but that doesn't just give him the right to intrude in my personal space like this.

Cloaked in darkness, like it is his favourite place to hide. No, not hide, watch and wait. Like a predatory animal hunting in its natural habitat.

"What are you doing in here? This is my room." My words are angry, and I spit them like sniper bullets. Yet I can't help the way my eyes drop to his long, muscular arms that drape along the armrests.

The light from the fire highlights his muscular forearms and the corded veins that rope under his skin and disappear beneath his rolled-up sleeves.

Nixon hums his disagreement. Leaning forward, he rests his elbows on his knees. He is back in his black jeans and t-shirt, like he is the lead guitarist of a rock band and not the next Earl of Lennoxshire.

"They are all my rooms, Karina. You would do well to remember that." His dark eyes fix me in place. It is so dark in here, they appear like two black gems glistening in the firelight. But that's not what has my breath sticking in my throat.

Karina, not Miss Campbell. I like my name on his sinful lips more than I should.

I shift on my feet, and his eyes flash in the darkness. A wolfish grin cracks his lips, putting his white teeth on perfect display, and the only sound between us is the crackling from the logs on the fire.

"You won't be moving downstairs, Karina. You will be staying put, nice and close for my every beck and call. Who knows when I might need you. So, you can tell loverboy you won't be moving in next door to him for his convenience. You will be staying up here, *for mine.*"

The messed-up part is, out of everything that Nixon has just said, the only thing I want to chide him for is for calling Ryan my 'loverboy' because he isn't. We flirt, and yeah, we have hooked up a couple of times to scratch an itch we can't get from anywhere else in this secluded location, but by no means are we in love, or even an item.

Yet I keep my mouth shut. Eyeing him from head to toe in both fear and appreciation. Nixon is an enigma; he doesn't have to go out of his way to possess your full attention. It happens naturally with the way he moves and the inexplicable presence that radiates from him. I want to step away from the fireplace, my body burning up now for a completely different reason, but to make a move would make my current predicament obvious even to a blind man, never mind someone as perceptive as Nixon.

"Don't sit out there again." He throws his hand in the direction of the window that overlooks the bridge outside, his brows drawn in what could be mistaken for concern if I didn't know him better. "I allowed that as a one-off, but if I catch you sitting on that bridge again, I will have them tear it down."

He pushes to his full height and stalks slowly towards me. My mouth dries in anticipation, yet my pride is doing anything that it can to conceal the effect that he has on me. "Are you worried about me?" I sass as best as I can, despite my word vomit.

He hums again in that deliciously deep voice that hits me right between the legs. "More like I don't want you getting ill or falling into the loch, causing you to call in sick on your first day."

He lifts one of his hands, yet stops as it reaches my face. His ring glints with the reflection of the fire and, for a moment, I think that he is either going to cuff my throat or tuck a stray strand of hair behind my ear like he has done before. I am ashamed to admit to myself, even for a second, that as I hold my breath, I hope it is the former. Instead, he drops his hand and makes a quick beeline for the door. I stare at his retreating form with shameful disappointment, at a loss for words as realisation sinks in.

Nixon is the one who lit the fire for me.

He doesn't stop or turn as he calls in a deep, commanding voice, "See you at six tomorrow. Bright and early, in my father's old office."

Nixon doesn't wait to hear my reply, but he doesn't have to. I have a feeling the new 16th Earl of Lennoxshire is used to getting what he wants, one way or another.

Four

Karina

He is staying.

I suspected that he might, but I hoped with everything in me that he wouldn't.

Yet here we are. I have spent my whole morning unpacking boxes that have been sent from his penthouse in London—at an alarmingly fast pace, may I add. I have reorganised his wardrobe, since the last time he lived here when he was a young teen. So, his old belongings have been condensed into a corner in the monstrous space, and I am currently hanging all his newly delivered clothes from occasion to casual wear. However, there isn't much variety. Mostly black denims and neutral tees, or black slacks and white button-down shirts. I have placed his many pairs of leather dress shoes and trainers in order of occasion. I scoff, looking at the soles. Most of them look like they have been worn twice at a push.

I have a feeling he asked for more items than he intended to wear to be sent to Scotland, with having me organising them in mind. The grin on his face when he gave me my task was nothing short of boyish delight.

It was alarmingly adorable.

It feels intrusive being in Nixon's intimate space. He has only been here for a few days, yet the room is already saturated with his presence. Embarrassingly, I am fascinated, my fingertips gently dancing over each item individually, as I tiptoe around his en suite. Bottles of Dior Sauvage and Tom Ford shaving products are scattered haphazardly across his marble bathroom counter. The wet razor sits beside his black electric toothbrush, both showing signs of recent use. My eyes roll when I come across a pair of black nail clippers, and I chuckle to myself.

Even his bloody nail clippers need to be chic.

The music in my headphones lowers, and a ping alerts me to a new message.

Nixon: Once you're finished, come to the library.

My outstretched hand snaps back to my side, and I glance around. Paranoid that Nixon knows what I have been doing lurking around in his bathroom, like some sort of creepy stalker.

I check my appearance in his vanity, noting with reluctance that the colour in my cheeks has returned for the first time since my mother passed. My chest feels lighter too, and I hate to admit it, but I have a feeling that Nixon's arrival, albeit an unwelcome one, has been a good distraction from the worries that burden me even in my dreams.

Taking one last look around his domain, I decide it is best I leave. His residual presence lingers heavily in this room and it's infecting me through osmosis. It is intoxicating, gradual and without any effort on his part, and if I spend any longer in here, I fear I will be incurable.

My footsteps slow as I approach the double doors of the library. Loud music blares from behind the engraved antique wood. Cautiously, I push them wide with both hands and stop in confusion at the sight before me.

The library is almost unrecognisable. The priceless antique furniture has been pushed aside and, in its place, large metal work desks filled with computer screens take up the centre of the room. Nixon stands behind a chair, leaning over a setup that consists of three computer screens on a triple monitor stand. He is typing rapidly on his phone as Bring me the Horizon blares from the speakers near the window. I step further into the room, past open laptops that seem to be in the process of downloading, with my jaw slack.

The contrast between old and modern is so shocking it is almost laughable. The room is like a visual representation of the man himself. Nixon stands before me in his usual black jeans and t-shirt, working away as though the music in here isn't loud enough to rival a rock concert. His hair is long enough at the top, that with his head dipped, a few messy strands hang over his eyes. If you didn't know Nixon, and you walked in on him like this, you would never suspect that he is part of the gentry.

Right now, he looks like a punk from the wrong side of the tracks. Until he opens his mouth, that is, and his perfectly spoken English, laced with a Scottish accent from his past, tells you that he was educated in the finest schools in the land.

Nixon glances over his shoulder as I enter the room, continuing a conversation that I can't make out over the music. He tracks me as I move around the edges of the room behind the monitors, which load up information I cannot make sense of, to the old bookcases as I examine the rows of classics. Everything from Tolstoy and Jane Austin to Allan Edgar Poe.

"Do you read?" His heat radiates into my back as he appears like a silent killer, despite turning the music low until it is nothing more than background noise.

I stop tracing the bound spines and spin to face him. "Not really. I would prefer old records to books."

He flashes another one of his boyish grins. "Yeah, me too."

"Maybe you can turn one of the rooms into a music library?" I suggest, breaking eye contact. His eyes are too intense sometimes, like he is trying to read my mind with one penetrative stare.

He laughs, humourless, all traces of the smile wiped from his face. "Maybe the next owner can do that."

"Next owner." My feet take me closer to him without thought. "What are you talking about?"

"This place will be going up for sale in the new year." He bends down and examines a laptop at his side, clicking as he talks. "I will give the farmers a chance to buy their land. It only seems fair, as some of them have farmed that land for generations. If they don't want to, or do not have the means, then I will sell their land."

"Nixon, you cannot be serious."

"Frankly, it is none of your business, Miss Campbell." Nixon casts me a stony glance, and it couldn't be more obvious that my input in less than wanted. However, I can't stop myself. To strip the Lennox estate down to the bones would be a travesty.

"And the staff, Maggie, Ryan and everyone else, what will they do?" I implore him with my eyes wide, but Nixon doesn't spare me a second glance. Why would he? As far as he is concerned, his word is final, and his opinion is the only one that matters.

"I don't give a shit. Now, since I will be working from here for the foreseeable future, I need better service speed. The Wi-Fi here is dire. My mate from London will be arriving tomorrow to update everything. I need you to set up a room. Make sure it is in the east wing. I do not want to listen to him, as he can get rather rowdy after hours."

"Nixon!" I beg him to listen. How can he be so heartless? This has been his family home for generations and people's livelihoods depend on him. "Please, think about this. You are upset. You have just lost your father, and you are not in a fit state of mind to be making rash decisions like this."

He pounces on me then, stepping into my body and walking us backwards with nothing but the pressure of his chest against mine. My back hits the wall of books, and the air leaves my lungs in a whoosh. One of his powerful hands whips up from his side, and unlike last night, I flinch. I expect him to grab me by the jaw or throat, but instead he grips the shelf above my head.

Leaning down, he dips his chin until he is at my eye level. "Do not presume to know me or my state of mind, *Karina*." He hisses my name like it is poison on his lips. My chest heaves and, despite myself, my head grows foggy as I inhale lungful after lungful of his intoxicating scent. "I am still digging around on you and the hold you had on my father, so don't get too comfortable. You should spend more time worrying about yourself than other people."

His eyes drop to my mouth and his eyelids get heavy. His dark lashes fan over his sharp cheekbones, and I almost whimper at how beautiful he is. It is cruel that someone so breathtaking can be so inhumane.

Nixon lifts his other hand and strokes the hair off my cheek and tucks it behind my ear with a gentleness he doesn't seem capable of. A shiver runs down my spine, and I close my eyes in an effort to get my head on straight.

"Scared, or turned on?" the cocky bastard has the audacity to ask.

Yet my feet remain planted, and I can't seem to find the strength to push him away.

Dipping his head into the crook of my neck, he hums as he takes a deep breath of my skin and the hair that covers it. "Yeah." A sadistic chuckle fills the air. "You should definitely be more concerned for yourself."

He pushes off me like he has been shocked and is back busying himself at one of his many computers, like I am no longer in the room, while I stand frozen on the spot like a statue.

I come to my senses and make out of the room on shaky legs. Cursing myself internally for my weakness and lapse of judgement. I would promise that it will never happen again, but deep down, I know that would make me a liar.

Nixon is bad news. In every sense. Hotter than sin and not the kind of guy you can mess around with casually and escape in one piece. It does not take a genius to work that one out. And clearly, I am a fool, because I would have just let him ravish me against the bookshelf in broad daylight.

"We will dine at six o'clock, Miss Campbell." I stop in my tracks at his words, dread filling me as I realise that he is enjoying torturing me. "Yoga pants are not suitable attire for the formal dining room, so please find something more appropriate to wear this evening."

I storm out, slamming the priceless door behind me, almost certain I hear a frustrated growl and a crash of heavy books from the other side before the music is turned up to full volume once again.

Five

Nixon

Another minute late, and I will be ready to drag her out of her room, dressed or not.

Karina arrives at twenty past six. Like I knew she would, her small way of saying that she isn't standing about, waiting for my next order, but that does not mean I enjoy being kept waiting.

Of course, she was worth the wait, though. Tight leather trousers that hug her thighs and ass and put them on perfect display steal my attention as she moves towards me, and I narrow my eyes at the black corseted top that accentuates her already tiny waist and subtly emphasizes her cleavage.

Dragging my eyes up to her face, she flashes me a cocky smile of her own.

Yeah, she is trying to distract me on purpose.

Little brat.

Standing before she arrives at my side, I pull her chair out for her, the same as last time, mostly because I love seeing the shock on her face. My manners surprise her, which is quite sad when I think about it. Either chivalry is dead, or she truly believes I am an uncivilised beast incapable of even the most basic of manners.

I asked Maggie to make Karina's favourite dishes for dinner this evening. My aim is to make her comfortable before pulling the rug out from beneath her feet.

As I had hoped, a small smile caresses her lips when she spots the lentil soup and freshly baked crusty bread laid out. I push her chair in easily since she is a little slight thing, before leaning over her body. Bringing my face close to her ear, I reach out and pull the cloth napkin off the table. Karina reaches out, expecting me to hand it to her, but instead I bypass her hand and let the fabric drop open, bringing my hand around her other side so that she is now bracketed in my loose embrace as I catch hold of the other corner and slowly drape the cream material across her lap. I linger a second longer than is proper, breathing in her perfume and shampoo. An intoxicating mix of jasmine and peaches.

"You look beautiful this evening." My truthful words are whispered like a secret, despite us being the only two people in this vast room.

Karina clears her throat and moves her head away from me, but I don't miss the shiver that runs down her spine at the caress of my breath.

I have never spoken words so true either. Karina Campbell is a thing of beauty, a 'bonnie wee queen' as they would say in these parts. A pretty young lady she is, indeed, her pale, unblemished skin offset by her bright red hair and eyes as blue as the freshwater springs at the foot of the Lennox Mountains.

"Your hair," I enquire. "Is that your natural colour?"

She fidgets in her chair before bringing her hand to sweep her hair off her bare shoulders. "Yes, I have thought about covering it up with dye many times over the years, but I could never bring myself to do it."

"Why?" My heart beats faster at the mere thought of her changing it. Her hair is exquisite.

"A highland cow." Her voice is such a low mumble. I laugh, sure that I heard her wrong.

Her eyes flare and lock on mine. "Don't laugh, asshole!"

Holding my hand out in surrender, I try my best to curb my laughter. "I'm sorry, I just thought I heard you say it was the same colour as a highland cow."

"I did." She continues staring at me. Daring me to react the same way twice, only when she is satisfied that I won't does she continue. "When I was younger, all the kids used to laugh and moo at me. They said I had hair like a highland cow."

My head rears back, realising that she is serious. "Give me their full names and dates of birth. I will have their bank accounts emptied and lives destroyed in minutes. Just say the word."

Karina laughs gently and lifts her cutlery. She thinks that I am joking, but I guess it is because she has no clue what business I am in. I decide to go against my nature and change the tone. "Kids are little fuckers, and your hair is beautiful. I'm glad that you never let them change you."

"Thank you, that is very...kind."

"I, for one, love highland cows. Magnificent beasts." I shove an oversized lump of bread in my mouth and smile around it.

Karina stares at me, her big eyes round and wide, before she bursts into a fit of laughter. It is as though she has just realised how ridiculous the whole notion is and, for the first time, my heart warms at the thought of being the one who could do that for her.

"Take a walk with me," I ask her as our plates are being cleared, unsure of my motives.

I am still suspicious of her reasons for being here, but I am captivated by her. Something about her intrigues me beyond measure in a way that I have never experienced.

In the cloakroom, we bundle into our winter coats and boots. The first snow of the season fell today, and my gut tells me that we are in for a bad winter. Still, the grounds are beautiful when they have been dusted with snow, and it has been years since I explored my old hunting grounds.

We make our way around the back, walking in comfortable silence, each of us enjoying the quiet peace that the night brings while taking in the crisp night air. Karina stares up at the stars, lost in her own thoughts, and I fall back a little slip behind a tree, admiring her as her boots crunch in the snow and the slight wind blows her hair across her delicate face.

After a few minutes, she stops and casts eyes like Bambi around her, realising I am no longer beside her.

"Nixon?" Her soft voice travels across the untouched snow and echoes around the trees.

With nothing but the moonlight and the glow from the house in the distance to help her see, she shifts on her feet.

"Stop playing, Nixon. Get out here." Her voice is firm, but her eyes flicker with uncertainty.

Am I playing? Karina doesn't know me well enough to be certain.

Finding a fallen branch, I step on it, so it crunches under my boot, and I crouch low, putting my hand in the snow.

Karina's eyes zero in on the direction of the noise and the tree that I hide behind, but her steps carry her slowly backwards in retreat. I stand tall to my full height and step out from behind the tree. Collar pulled high, and my head dipped, I look at her through my lashes. Tucking my hands behind my back, I threaten her in a low, cold voice.

"I would run if I were you." Confusion, followed by fear, pulls at her face and she is frozen to the spot, like the deer that we hunt only a mile from here.

With careful and deliberate movements, I draw my hands from behind my back, revealing two perfectly formed snowballs. Her chest exhales with relief before her eyes immediately twinkle with glee.

Arching a brow at her, silently daring her to stay and fight, she squeals with delight as she rushes off behind a cluster of trees, thinking that it will protect her.

It won't.

But I am thrilled that she has chosen to run, as I am going to take great pleasure in hunting her down. I launch the snow at the trunk of the tree that she hides behind, causing her to scream, before I slip off in the opposite direction to hide and wait once again.

After a few minutes, I watch as Karina peeks her head out from behind the tree and makes a dash in my direction. Having no idea that she is running right into my clutches.

I silently round the tree, and she takes up the spot that I have just vacated, and we are separated by nothing but the thick tree trunk. We are so close, I can hear her panting with excitement and exertion. Reaching out a hand, I stroke the bark as if it was her body.

"Think, Karina, think." Her sweet voice sounds right in my ear, and she has no clue.

Crouching down, I quickly make another round of snowballs, cradling them in my hands as I sneak off to the side while she is busy hiding.

I throw a decoy, with the intention of pulling her out of her hiding spot so that I can catch her on the other side.

It works, and I watch as she dashes across the snow, her red hair flowing behind her and laughing the whole time. I launch my last two balls, as she spins while simultaneously throwing one of her own, hitting me on the chest as we both hit our targets perfectly.

Shit, she has good aim.

Grinning to myself, I drop lower to the ground and collect more ammo, assuming now that she is doing the same. My heart pumps with adrenaline and the thrill of the chase.

God, I haven't felt this alive in years.

Time to collect my reward.

Pushing up, I prowl in her direction, and she screams when she sees me coming, launching snowballs one after the other as quickly as she can make them. Karina doesn't miss a shot, but that doesn't deter me, so she makes a last-minute dash when I am within reach. But she isn't quick enough to escape me. My fingers wrap around her nape, and I drag her into my body, her small hands landing on my chest and fisting my coat as she crashes into me.

"The spoils of war," I purr with satisfaction as I run my hand into the back of her hair and pull her mouth towards mine. Her lips are cold on mine, but her hot tongue slips out, demanding entrance. And who am I to deny her.

Pressing my fingers against the pulse point on her neck, I find it galloping at lightning speed. "Scared?" I pull back, my mouth sliding across hers. "Or turned on?" I repeat my words from earlier today. If I had to guess, I would say both, and I would bet that it is a combination that she enjoys.

Standing on her tiptoes, she pushes closer to me, testing the hold I have on her hair, and she moans against my lips as she wraps her arms around my neck, clearly enjoying the sting from her scalp.

Not so innocent, after all. My mind races at the thought of how deep her still waters run. Breaking the kiss, I press my forehead to hers and cup her jaw with my free hand. Spreading my fingers wide, I push my thumb over her plump lips and dip it into her mouth, and to my delight, she opens her mouth wide. Her blue eyes glitter in the moonlight when I press the pad down on her tongue. I practically growl as her eyelids drop heavily and full of lust. Karina lets her head fall backwards, her forehead leaving mine to give me better access. With my fist full of her hair, I tug a little more until her neck is stretched completely. I follow closely, staying within a whisper of a breath the whole time. I remove my thumb and slide two fingers into her hot little mouth, as she bares her teeth in a seductive smile and encloses my fingers between lips. I am so much bigger than her, and my fingers hit the back of her throat mercilessly, giving her a taste of how things would be if we were to take things further, yet she stares me dead in the eye and swallows everything I give her.

My fingers are practically down her throat, putting her gag reflex to the test, her hair in my tight hold, and I have her completely at my mercy. She can't break free unless I allow it. Yet, something is pulling in my gut, telling me that Karina is the one in control.

My face may be a perfected mask of indifference, yet my heart is pounding wildly in its confines. My mouth is watering with the desire to devour her without restraint, and in a way, that would confirm I have no control whatsoever when it comes to her.

Now, let the record state that this has never happened in my entire twenty-five years. Karina may be the one in the compromised position, but the way she groans around my fingers while her eyes blaze in a silent challenge has me breathing in short, laboured breaths like it is her hands that are closing around my throat.

I need to get this shit under control and sort my head out. She is still hiding something from me, and I need to figure it out before she gets the upper hand.

I dip my mouth to the corner of hers and chuckle humourlessly. She quickly senses the change in me, her body turning from pliant to stiff in my grasp in seconds.

"My, my, Miss Campbell. It seems that you know how to play better than I assumed. Congratulations, you have officially piqued my interest." I lick the side of her neck slowly and stop at the shell of her ear, keeping my voice as quiet at the falling snow around us. "That won't be a good thing for you."

I release her, and she stumbles, quickly breaking out of the trance we shared only seconds before. Her blue eyes wide and thoroughly pissed off.

Good, that means I am getting to her, slicing through her carefully spun web of lies.

"We are done for this evening." I dismiss her and pull my phone out of my pocket to busy myself; otherwise, I might drag her back behind the tree to finish what we started. "And don't even think about finding Ryan to scratch that itch I just created. Straight to your room. I will know if you do anything different, and it will be Ryan who pays for your disobedience."

Karina narrows her eyes, and her lips twist with what I am sure is a mouthful of abuse.

Huffing, she stomps past me in the direction of the house, the wind whipping her hair like burning flames across my face as a parting *fuck you,* but I keep my head down, follow her only with my eyes, ensuring she makes it inside the house.

Squeezing the truth out of the lying little temptress is going to be the most fun I have had in years.

Six

Karina

For a castle, it is surprisingly cosy. Once again, my fire had been lit for me, and after a hot bath, I slip under the fleece-lined duvet.

I try to watch Netflix on my laptop, but it keeps buffering, and I don't need a computer degree to tell me that the excessive amount of tech that Nixon is having rigged up downstairs is to blame.

Slamming the screen closed, I stare at the ceiling, restless. My skin is buzzing underneath with an energy I can't describe. It is like an itch that I am dying to scratch, but I know I can't relieve it myself. If I didn't know any better, I would say I am horny. That the little stunt in the forest with Nixon has left me sexually frustrated, but I refuse to admit that he has that kind of effect on my body.

You could have gone to Ryan's room, but you didn't.

My conscience taunts me, proving just how much control Nixon has over me right now.

A smile splits my lips at the memory of my effect on him, though. He wasn't expecting me to meet him head on tonight. He thought I would run away at his advances. In fact, I bet he was counting on it. Nixon thought it would be a simple task to chase me out of his castle.

I am afraid for him it will not be as easy as that. Right now, I don't have anywhere else to be but here. But when the time is right, I will go, far away from here, and Nixon will never see my face again.

My stomach dips at the thought, and I question my sanity.

He created the itch, and like the tease he is, didn't follow through, and to add insult to injury, he then forbade me from seeking relief elsewhere.

Dick.

An idea comes to me, and I can't help the absurdity of it, yet I never was one to listen to good advice.

I pull up the text with Nixon and study the photograph beside his name. It is a picture of a sunset and the little green dot at the bottom tells me that he is online.

I text a few words and then quickly delete them. Changing my mind several times about what to say.

Nixon: Cat got your tongue?

My heart jumps when a message from Nixon pings up on the screen.

Me: Excuse me?

Nixon: You have been 'typing' for about five minutes. At least it confirms that you are not in Ryan's bed right now and you are in your own.

Me: Hmm, how do you know that I have not already been to his bed, and now back in my own?

Nixon: Well, for one, I sent him out on a job this evening, and secondly, if you are used to spending less than an hour in his bed, then Ryan must be more disappointing in the sack than I thought.

This guy! He sent Ryan away for the night to ensure that I stayed away from him.

Me: Ryan is anything but disappointing in bed.

Nixon: Not what the clock says sweetheart.

Me: Yeah, well, maybe it just means that he is so skilled he gets me off in record time.

Nixon: Maybe...

The audacity of this man. What the hell does he know?

Nixon: Or maybe you have just confirmed how disappointing he is.

Me: ?

Nixon: One quickie wouldn't even be close to enough for me.

Me: Oh, look, Nixon Lennox acting like he can go all night.

Although something tells me that he most definitely can.

Nixon: Maybe not ALL night. But long enough that you wouldn't have enough strength to walk the next morning. And that your muscles would be left with a delicious ache that would remind you of me with every move you made.

Oh shit, that's hot. I squeeze my thighs together at the thought of a guy like Nixon working my body over and over until our limbs were a tangled, sweaty mess.

Me: Yeah, yeah, that's what they all say, Big shot!

Nixon: I am sure that it is. Tell me, Karina, have you been left disappointed much in the past?

Me: I know what you're doing.

Nixon: ?

Me: Have I been disappointed in the past? Yes. Recently? No, I have been VERY satisfied recently.

Nixon: Is that why you are wet and needy right now, thinking about how I would feel between your legs tonight, Karina?

My eyes flutter closed. It is like I can hear him whispering my name in my ear, in his gravelly voice that is threatening and sensual all at once.

This game I am about to play is a dangerous one. But those ones are always the most fun.

I reply before I have a chance to talk myself down.

Me: Nothing that my hand can't fix

Nixon: Karina...

Me: Yes, Nixon?

Nixon: Don't play with me.

Me: But it's fun to play, don't you think?

Nixon: Let me warn you now, Karina. I am not a casual man. I don't play nicely, I don't play fair, and I most definitely do not share.

Me: Hmm, talk is cheap.

My hand trembles slightly as I grip my phone, holding my breath as I wait for his reply. Maybe he has changed his mind, or he was teasing me to see how far I would take this. Using this as a ploy to get me out of his house.

My mind is racing and my eyes blur as I look at the screen, rereading our conversation several times.

There is a knock at the door, and my heart falls into my stomach. I don't need to answer it to know that Nixon is standing on the other side. I can feel his untamed energy radiating through the wood.

I slide out of bed and stand in the middle of the room, weighing up the consequences of opening it or leaving him out there. But I don't get time to decide. The next thing I know, the door handle rattles, and the door swings open. Nixon steps over the threshold like a dark vampire prince who has been invited and can now enter whenever he wishes.

"Get on the fucking bed." His dark eyes rake over me slowly, thoroughly inspecting me.

"Nixon." My voice is nothing more than a breathy whisper.

"On the bed, legs spread wide and your hands above your head. Now," he commands, his voice sounding rougher than usual.

I think about refusing. But my legs move from their own desire, and I step backwards until my knees hit the edge of the bed.

Nixon's dark eyes, raw with possession, track my every move. He is still dressed in the same clothes from dinner, and it's a stark contrast to my silk sleep shorts and vest.

Nixon nods once in the direction of the bed, the muscles in his jaw flexing as he wordlessly instructs me to lie back. I turn around and crawl across the mattress, giving him a clear view of my behind as I climb up and lie down on the pillows. Crossing my wrists above my head, I take one final deep breath and open my legs.

"Wider." I can't look at him as he moves closer.

The pyjamas are covering my most intimate parts, yet I have never felt more exposed as I follow his instructions. Nixon steps up to the foot of the bed, and I finally raise my eyes to meet his. His pupils are so blown out, his eyes appear almost black, and like a demon of the night, threaten to swallow me whole.

Standing there in a creased white shirt and black slacks, raven hair falling over his eyes, and cheekbones as sharp as his tongue, he looks like Satan himself. A wicked angel who will promise you the greatest pleasures in life, if only you pledge your soul in return.

And me? I spread my legs wider in anticipation. Giving him my full surrender and permission to do with me as he wishes.

I question my sanity for a second, and Nixon must notice, because a devilish smirk twists the side of his red lips. Yet, instead of being perturbed, I can think of nothing other than how much I want that mouth in places I would never admit out loud. I think I actually whimper at the thought, but I can't be sure. All I can hear is my blood whooshing frantically in my ears.

Wetness is pooling between my legs, and my nipples ache as they rub shamelessly against my silk camisole, not giving me nearly enough friction. I watch as Nixon painstakingly rolls his shirt sleeves up his muscled forearms.

"You are going to be a good girl for me, aren't you, Karina?" It is not a question; it is a warning.

My mouth is too dry for words, so I nod my reply instead.

Leaving the foot of the bed, Nixon drags the back of his fingertips from my foot and up the inside of my leg, moving casually as though he is admiring a painting in a museum. He arrives at my side, dragging his hand across my stomach and up between my breasts, arriving at my neck, which he gently collars with his warm hand.

I use everything to try to steady my breaths, but I am seconds away from panting like a mare after a hard ride.

He hasn't even got started.

His calloused fingers trace a path downward, pulling the silk until it rests under my breasts. Humming his approval, a blush works its way up my chest. Pleased at seemingly having passed his inspection.

Touch me! I repeat the words over and over in my head. Too ashamed to say them out loud, but to my disappointment, Nixon moves away back to the foot of the bed. My hips grind into the bed, desperately trying to give myself some sort of relief.

Without warning, Nixon grabs my ankles and drags me down the bed. He doesn't stop until my hips are hanging off the end, and throws my legs over his shoulders. His tongue slips out, wetting his full bottom lip.

"Nixon!" I plead, desperately hoping that he will finally touch me.

He slides my shorts to the side, exposing me completely and buries his head between my legs, covering my centre entirely with his mouth.

I throw my head back and groan his name, not caring if the entire house hears. Nixon eats me like I am the best thing that he has ever tasted, swiping his tongue from back to front, licking and sucking at my lips. I barely remember to breathe as he spreads me wide with his strong fingers and flicks my clit relentlessly with his skilled tongue, before sliding down and teasing my opening. His sinful mouth is hot and wet, and I thrash and moan on the bed as he plunges his tongue inside my pussy before pulling out and swirling my clit again with maddening delicacy. The depraved noises we are making together leave no doubt about what is happening in here.

My hands twist in his thick hair, and I grind shamelessly into his face, desperate for the orgasm I can feel cresting. And then he stops.

"Nixon?"

"Hands above your head, baby, or I stop." My hands can't hit the mattress quick enough, and he laughs darkly as his mouth returns to my sensitive lips. "Good choice. Now come on my face, pretty girl, and I might just give you my cock too."

"Oh God!" His fingers bite into my sensitive skin as he holds me wide open.

"God's not here, Karina. Moan *my* name and let everyone hear who is pleasing this perfect little pussy. Let Ryan know who's feasting on this cunt."

My eyes roll shut in euphoria as Nixon pushes two fingers inside of me just as he sucks my clit into his mouth and grazes it gently with his teeth. My insides pulse, my entire body coming alive as I chant his name on repeat, I don't care who hears as one orgasm rolls into another until I lose count.

Holy hell, he wasn't all talk after all.

I don't have an ounce of energy to move from this position. A satisfied sigh passes my lips, and my eyes drift closed. I don't think I would be able to tell you my own name right now if you asked.

Somewhere I register Nixon sliding me back to the top on the bed and covering me with the bed throw.

"I will be back for my main course, pretty girl. Rest up; I won't be long."

He leaves, and I fall into a dreamless sleep, unburdened by worries or troubles. For the first time in a long time.

Seven

Nixon

I lick the taste of her from my lips.

My phone had been vibrating in my pocket the entire time I had my face buried between Karina's heavenly thighs. Pulling my focus in opposing directions, I am desperate to spend the night buried inside of Karina's perfect cunt, yet a few hours ago, after I sent her back indoors from our tryst in the snow, I called my private investigator.

I have told him to leave no stone unturned in order to dig up any dirt on Karina. She is hiding something. I can feel it in my bones. My motives have changed. I have no desire to cast her out into the cold. Quite the opposite, in fact. I need to know that I am not inviting a venomous serpent into my bed.

So, the timing may be frustrating for me, but little does he know, it couldn't have been timed any better.

My hearts speeds as the dial tone rings. The information he has for me will dictate how the rest of my evening goes.

"Nixon, sorry if I have called at a bad time."

"What have you got for me?" I don't give a fuck about pleasantries. I need to know what he knows. Now.

"Karina Campbell, twenty-one years of age. Grew up in Glasgow, raised by her mother who died two years ago, no father or any other family on record. Was attending Glasgow College of Nursing before moving to Lennox House to care for your father. No criminal record, not even a parking ticket. She looks squeaky clean, if you don't count the fact that she was sleeping with one of her college professors."

Hmm... interesting. "How old is he?" My curiosity gets the better of me, and I curse myself internally.

This search for information is not because I am on the lookout to be the next crazy stalker boyfriend. But Karina doesn't strike me as the kind of girl who would suck her professor off for a good grade.

Was he forcing himself on her, abusing his power?

"David Stewart, Pharmacy Professor, aged forty-one, sir." He clears his throat, getting uncomfortable with my motives.

"Has he tried contacting her?" I pull out a tumbler and pour two fingers of a cheap whisky that sits on the countertop.

"I doubt it. She changed her phone the day that she moved to Lennox House."

"What do you mean?"

"I mean, if I had to guess, I would say that she didn't want anyone from back home contacting her."

Why on earth would she want that?

"Okay, good work. Keep me updated."

I hang up the phone before he has a chance to reply, and spin towards the sink to dispose of the glass. It is then I notice Ryan is sitting in the dark at the table, nursing a whiskey of his own. I narrow my eyes, annoyed I didn't notice him sooner, analysing his expression to judge how much of my conversation that he has heard.

I lied to Karina earlier. I hadn't sent Ryan away this evening, and I am glad that I never did. I hope he heard us together in her bedroom. The building is vast, but the large, cavernous hallways carry sound like an opera theatre.

"So, the king of the manor hasn't wasted any time bedding the servants." His insulting words roll over one another, making it blatant that isn't his first drink of the evening.

I pace along the kitchen, tracing my fingers over a bowl of fruit, and give him a knowing smirk.

He heard.

Excellent.

I refrain from answering him, knowing he has more to say, and happy to let him get it all out and to show me his cards.

"Karina isn't the type of girl you just bed and don't call the next day. If you have no intentions with her, then let her go. Set her free from whatever game it is you are playing here, Lennox."

"Oh, I have plenty of *intentions* with Miss Campbell, I can assure you of that. And it seems she is a fan of the kind of games that I like to play." It is too easy to antagonise him, and the sick bastard I am, I revel in it.

"I have known you since we were infants, Nixon. I remember how short your attention span was with all the recreational activities you indulged in. Riding, shooting, fencing, girls—it didn't matter. Once you mastered them, you got bored and quickly moved on to the next distraction."

"I am glad you can admit my superior talents." My smile is humourless and laced with malice. Ryan has no idea that the reason I kept myself busy in our youth was to keep off my father's radar. The less that I was in the house, the less he could find me to *discipline* me.

Sluggishly, he pushes off the table and stands to his unsteady feet. "I mean it, you bastard, leave her out of whatever axe it is that you are here to grind. I won't back off! Karina doesn't want me to."

"Just because we have known one another since we were children, Ryan, do not take that as a free pass. I will throw you off this land quicker than you can blink. I have no care for loyalty towards you, your father, or for the number of years that the Mackenzie family has worked for this estate. If you get in my way with Karina, it will be as though you never existed here."

"Should Karina not be the one to choose?" He tips his chin in defiance, playing to the competitive side he knows I possess in bucketloads.

I narrow my gaze and step up to the table, where we stand toe to toe in a face. Who the fuck does this prick think he is, threatening me in my own home? I *am* the king of this fucking castle, and he would do well to remember that. However, he may be right. What fun is it to take Karina unwillingly away from him. It would be so much more fun to witness his defeat as he watches her perky little arse crawl desperately to my bed.

That still doesn't mean that I would have to play fair. I almost agree to his terms, but then the thought of anyone other than me sinking their claws into her or tasting her makes my skin feel like it has been doused in gasoline and set alight.

I refuse to share or give her up until I have devoured her.

Karina is *mine,* and I will not stop until I possess her mind, body and soul. Until she can't take her next breath without an unquenchable thirst for me and the things that I do to her.

Fuck Ryan and his limp dick. He can have her back once I am done with her.

"Touch her and see what happens." My warning is the last thing I gave him before striding out of the kitchen and back in search of the woman in question.

Let's just see how loud I can make her cry out my name this time. I have all night to drive him to the breaking point of insanity.

***

I close the mahogany door with a quiet click. I didn't come straight here, stopping by my new set up in the library first, and I assume that Karina has fallen into a deep and satisfied slumber. I wanted to come sooner; however, I have a very important client who is waiting for a new firewall I have designed for his company. It is of high importance, as his business isn't exactly legal. Avi Salvadore is the head of the Boston Mafia, and my particular skill set was recommended to him by one of his associates I also do business with in London. It took some time for me to gain access to his inner circle, but I have been compensated handsomely for my discretion.

A buddy of mine once asked if I feel guilty about working with the unsavoury types I do business with and, in all honestly, I couldn't help but laugh at him. The entire system of the British aristocracy is unsavoury. People just don't realise it, as we have had hundreds of years to hide and practice and pass laws that suit our best interests, to the point that joe blogs in the street doesn't even know ninety percent of the shit that goes on behind our gold-plated doors. At least criminals are upfront about who they are. Most of the time, anyway.

I think it is also part of the reason I want to get rid of this place. I don't want to continue the deceitful legacy, living under this title, which stands for so much that I despise. That is also another reason why I have worked so hard to stand on my own two feet. I never wanted to need this place or the privilege that it bequeaths me.

But I digress, and the woman lying in the bed before me is the most perfect distraction for my maddening thoughts.

It is impossible not to admire the goddess before me, lying on her side, her auburn hair fanning across her pale face and silk pillow. The dips of her body obvious underneath the throw exactly where I left her, although the material has slid down to reveal the outside curve of her breast, which rises and falls in a slow, hypnotic rhythm.

Debating if I should let her sleep a little longer and take a shower, I realise with reluctance that I can't move from my spot. Watching her in this peaceful state is captivating. Karina is such a mystery to me, and I bathe in the luxury of the small insight into her private and vulnerable state. I have gotten used to battling her and the guard she walks around with constantly that I am entranced watching her in this new light.

Is it me and my presence here? Or has she grown up that way?

Her breathing changes and her body tenses. The change so subtle, I wouldn't have noticed if I wasn't watching her so intently.

Sleeping beauty is awake, and I can't help the smile that tugs the corner of my lips.

Karina knows that I am watching her sleep, and like a wild hare who is aware of a wolf in its midst, she thinks if she freezes, she will go unnoticed.

Too late, sweetheart, I have you locked in my sights now. No use trying to make a dash for freedom.

I stalk her, my feet carrying me to the foot of the bed. Karina's chest falls faster with every step closer to her. Bending at the hips, I place my palms on the bed, the mattress at her feet dipping with my weight.

"Ready to level up, little rabbit?" I purr to entice her, but my words hold enough of a threat that she continues her charade. "I know you're not sleeping, Karina."

I slip the cover to the side and circle her ankle, grazing her soft skin with the pad of my thumb. Desperate for her to be willing to continue the game we have started. A game where we will both be winners if she can let go and submit to our mutual desires.

"You know, I can still taste you on my tongue." My hand inches ever so slightly higher, and I keep my pressure so light, my skin is barely a whisper against hers. "You have the potential to be an addiction, Karina." My voice matches my touch, and she lets out the sexiest little sigh when my fingers reach the inside of her knee.

That is all the encouragement that I need and, in the blink of an eye, I scoop my hands under her thighs and drag her down the bed. Her fiery hair falls away, exposing her gorgeous face still soft with sleep. The lust obvious in her hooded eyes, and I damn near growl when I notice the evidence of my mouth in the marks along her collarbone and neck.

Fuck, they look good on her. In fact, I can't think of anything that would look better around her throat, not even millions of pounds' worth of the family diamonds.

Karina's bare legs drape off the end of the bed, at either side of mine. The fabric of my black slacks rubs against her naked skin. Her exposed pussy taunts me from below, but I keep my focus on her ocean eyes.

"Are you going to give me this body?" I slide my hands up her thighs and grip her hips. "One night to do as we wish with one another?" She is so small in my hands, I feel like I could crush her if I am not careful.

"Is that how a gentleman would ask?" Karina pushes up on her elbows, bringing our faces closer, and bats her thick lashes, but like the little minx that I am quickly realising she can be, she pushes her legs open a little wider beneath me.

Taunting me.

Inching my face closer, I skim my lips across hers. Her hot breath drifts into my open mouth, intoxicating me. I hum my disagreement before lifting my hand and cuffing her throat with a promise. "There is nothing gentlemanly about what I want to do to you, little rabbit. Now shut the fuck up and take this dick that I know you are so desperate for."

I sink my mouth into hers, swallowing her groan. I play with her mouth, licking and nibbling on her lips, before sliding my tongue over hers. It doesn't take long before our hands are forceful and roaming shamelessly, and we are both panting in anticipation.

Our kisses turn punishing, and I am practically eating her face, tasting everything that I can get my lips on. Karina tears my shirt open and slides it down my shoulders, pulling it off my body without ever breaking contact.

Fuck, she tastes good, and my cock is so fucking hard for her, I feel lightheaded from all the blood that must be gathered down there. The need to be inside of her is primal, and from the look on her flushed face and blown-out pupils, Karina is right there with me.

Taking one of her tits in my mouth, I fumble with my belt, letting it fall to the floor with my trousers, kicking everything away until I am as naked as the vixen beneath me.

With nothing left between us, I pull back and look down at the woman before me. Her red hair tousled and wild, her lips red from my assault. "Fuck, I want to do bad things to you," I groan hoarsely, more to myself than her.

I can't stand to wait a second longer. I guide her legs around my waist and press my length to her entrance. Her lips are slick with arousal and my mouth waters, knowing exactly how good she tastes down there. Karina wiggles her hips impatiently, and I grin at her neediness, before slowly pushing the tip of my dick inside.

We moan together at the snugness, and if I was a gentleman like she teased, I would take it slowly. But it's not who I am, nor is it what she wants from me, so I push forward, despite the tight fit until I bottom out, stretching her perfect little pussy to its limits.

Karina whimpers and claws at my shoulders but arches her back so that she can take all of me.

I dip my head, capturing her mouth once again. "Hm, I knew you would be a good girl for me," I taunt as I start to move inside of her.

She merely moans and returns my greedy kisses. "Are you sure that I am not the first one you have let in here?" I pant into her mouth, overwhelmed by how good she feels wrapped around me. "This is as tight as a little virgin pussy."

"Oh my god!" Her eyes roll closed, and she moves in time with my movements, as I grind slow and deep, making sure to hit all the spots inside of her. I suck and nip at the skin on her neck and shoulder, making sure to leave more of the marks that suit her so well. Our pleasure builds, and she bites down on my jaw, making me growl like a beast.

I pull out and glide my fingers over her slick folds before giving a flick of my wrist, and then a sharp tap, spanking her hot cunt until it twitches. "This might be the prettiest pussy that I have ever seen."

"Oh my god!" she chants again.

"It's Nixon, baby, and you're going to scream it nice and loud," I snarl in her ear. "I want to hear you beg for it."

I flip her onto her front and push back inside her in one thrust, pounding into her. Fucking her into the bed with the crazed possession of a madman. Sliding my hand through her thick mane, I twist her face, holding her steady as I capture her mouth, making sure to kiss her like I adore her while I am fucking her like I loathe her.

"I need more, Nixon. Please, give me more," she begs like a good girl against my lips, panting into my open mouth.

I rear back and pull her with me, settling her on all fours before sliding my hand down between us, parting my fingers until they are gliding around my dick as it slides in and out of her. My thumb now coated in our mess, it slips effortlessly over her clit as I flick back and forth.

She grinds into me harder and faster, and I grunt from the pleasure building rapidly in my groin. Fuck, I'm not sure how much longer I can hold on for. Karina's pussy is sweeter than heaven.

My muscles are burning as I pound into her over and over. Our bodies are slick with sweat, and the sound of skin hitting skin echoes around the room as she rotates her hips and slams back onto my cock, fucking me good and taking it all in return.

I wrap a hand around her throat, pulling her up on her knees until her back meets my chest. Long auburn hair tickles my skin when her head falls backwards and rests on my shoulder as I fuck up into her relentlessly.

Her tiny little fingers dig into my thighs and her body heats and tenses. "Mm, Nixon! Ugh, please, don't stop. Please!"

I tighten my hold on her throat and wrap my other arm around her, crushing her breasts under my forearm as I keep my strokes as steady as I can. Maintaining the rhythm that is pushing her over the edge. Her inner muscles contract, squeezing me impossibly tight, and I'm a goner. White light explodes behind my eyelids and her body squeezes me like a vise, making my strokes almost impossible as I unload inside of her. Groaning incoherent words of adoration, I fill her little pussy to the brim while it twitches around my cock, milking me until I am drained dry and dizzy.

We collapse on the bed, and I lie staring at the ceiling for a second, contemplating what I think might just have been the best sex I have ever had, when a giggle comes from the enchantress at my side.

"Well, that was fun." She rolls out of the bed, and I stop myself from reaching out and forbidding her from going wherever it is that she thinks she is going.

That's not what this is.

Karina struts naked and in her full radiant glory towards the bathroom before turning and looking at me over her shoulder. Long red hair falling to her waist like a siren, she dips a delicate hand between her legs, coats her fingers in the cum that is dripping out of her and locks eyes with me as she licks the skin clean. I stifle my groan and think about anything to stop my cock from hardening again, but it is futile.

"How about round two in the shower?" Without waiting for an answer, she disappears, leaving the door open, knowing full well that I will follow.

Eight

Karina

The house has been a different place all day.

Nixon's friend Jamieson arrived from London before breakfast and got to work right away. At the insistence of Nixon, I have no doubt. He brought a small team with him, but they are staying in one of the guest houses on one of the farms on the estate.

Noise and unfamiliar faces pour out of almost every room that I try to hide in, so I have sought refuge in the gardens. The fresh air will do me good anyway.

Last night was intense, and I do not regret a second of it; however, that doesn't mean I am filled with excitement at seeing Nixon in the harsh light of day.

Will he gloat?

Mock me?

Try to corner me and lure me into another round with the promise of countless mind-blowing, toe-curling orgasms?

More importantly, would I let him?

Delicious and addictive sex from an earthly god cannot distract me from my purpose here. This place is a steppingstone to get me where I need to be — as far away from Scotland as possible. I can't have any ties holding me back, or any crumbs as clues that I have even been here.

My mission to fly under the radar as much as possible has well and truly been blown to shit. Letting the lord of the manor fuck my brains out all night was not one of my wisest decisions, no matter how enjoyable it may have been.

I messed up, and I need to get my head back on straight.

Nixon has been locked in his office all morning with his tech guys, so he hasn't texted me once with any sort of demands or to-do lists. Not even a request for his usual morning coffee. Complete radio silence. Which does not surprise me, as I guess he does seem like the type to move on to the next pretty quickly. I can only imagine his lifestyle in London. I should be happy at the thought that last night means nothing to him, and the irregular thumping in my chest is from too much caffeine and too little sleep.

Nothing else.

The icy wind causes me to pull my coat tighter, and the trees rustle and swoosh in protest. I startle as a crow caws loudly before a large flock bursts through the treetops and disappears over the distinctive turrets that Lennox House is so greatly admired for. But there is something else that causes the hairs on the back of my neck to bristle. It is a strange feeling, one that you get when you know someone is watching you.

My adrenaline spikes, and I search the tree line, looking for something or someone and praying that I am overreacting or that sleep deprivation has made me hyper aware and edgy. Keeping my stance casual, I pull my phone out and pretend to type as I continue to search the grounds. There is nothing out of place, as tech guys come in and out, loading and unloading. Two of the usual gardeners run at their back, steering them clear of the pristine grass and flowerbeds, while the kitchen hands guide the food delivery around the back of the house.

Just as I dismiss my feeling of unease, something catches my eye in one of the large windows upstairs. Zeroing in, I notice Nixon. Leaning against the frame with what I assume is his usual double shot coffee in one hand, his head tilted as he tracks my every move.

How long has he been watching me? Is he the reason I could feel eyes on me?

Dressed in all black, matching his dark hair, he would almost be camouflaged in the shadows if it wasn't for his stark pale skin.

My phone vibrates, and I know it is him before I read the new message.

Nixon: I thought you would hide from me today.

Me: Looks like you are the one hiding.

Nixon: To my dismay, I have had business to attend to. Believe me, if I could spend all day between your thighs, I would.

Me: Wow, how romantic. You put Shakespeare to shame. You better watch out, if people find out you are such a poet, it could ruin your reputation.

Nixon: Worry not, darling, my reputation was ruined a long time ago.

I stare up at the window once again. His phone is in his hand, but he still has his eyes locked on me. Like he is more interested in what I will do next rather than what I will say.

Nixon: Regrets, Miss Campbell?

I'm a little stunned that he cares to ask.

Me: No.

It's all I manage, not willing to unpack my thoughts on what happened between us, and what I am sure with every minute that passes will happen again. I stare at him as he reads the message, and I think I see a small flicker of a smirk before he turns and fades into the darkness behind him.

A sickening mix of disappointment and trepidation swarms my gut, and I find myself rooted to the spot for a moment longer. Unsure of what to do or where to go, but knowing that the last thing I want to do is go back inside the house.

Into his domain. His castle, his territory, his lair.

"There you are," the familiar voice calls from behind, and I turn to face Ryan. "Still in one piece, I'm relieved to see."

Heat floods my cheeks, and I consider running for the hills. I have had enough of men today, and sitting on the bridge with my air pods turned to the max sounds exactly like the escape I need right now.

The look in his blue eyes tells me everything without asking.

He knows.

Guilt tingles my spine, and I shift on my feet. I know that I am not Ryan's girlfriend, but we have slept together a few times, probably would have again if it weren't for things with Nixon and me. He deserved a conversation before being intimate with someone else.

At the very least, as his friend. And his friendship here is something that I want to keep.

"Ryan," I sigh, unsure of the right words. "I eh…"

"Don't," he interrupts and steps into my space. Ryan dips his head and cups my face gently. "Do not apologise for getting caught in his deceitful web."

Gazing into his usually kind eyes, I find them sharp with hatred. "What do you mean?"

He continues without noticing how pissed off I am getting, too busy wrapped up in his own vendetta against someone he has probably viewed as competition his entire life. "I know how easy it is for men like him to ensnare young women like you."

"Women like me?" Is he for real right now? "And what kind of woman am I, Ryan?"

Finally, he snaps out of his haze and seems to consider his next words carefully. "You are kind and gentle, Karina. Much too decent and pure for a man like Nixon Lennox. His type can't help but seek to sully such goodness with their polluted minds because they know they will never deserve it."

"So, you think that you know what I deserve or who deserves me?" Ryan doesn't know me one ounce. He has no idea, and deep down, I don't think he is interested either. We had fun together, and I saw him as a good friend, yet he is quickly throwing that away due to pointless jealousy. This has nothing to do with him and I and everything to do with him and Nixon.

"Yes," he says with conviction.

"And that would be you?" My eyebrows almost reach my hairline.

Ryan stops, seeing what is happening here. "Karina, I would take good care of you. Don't throw what we have away for the thrill of bedding an Earl."

"You think so little of me." Giving him my back, I head in the direction of the house, ready to hide in my room for the rest of the day. Outdoors wasn't the safe haven I hoped that it would be.

"Karina!" Ryan's desperate voice is carried through the wind to my retreating form.

I don't stop, I won't until I have turned the lock on my bedroom door. "Go back to work, Ryan. We have said all that needs to be said for today."

My phone buzzes once again in my pocket, and I sigh inwardly. Nixon has likely spotted me talking to Ryan and has some more outlandish demands. Ones that I am no longer in the mood to fulfil.

Confusion twists my brows at the unknown number. I have a new phone, so only the staff at Lennox House have this number. It only takes seconds before the dread follows in the deepest pits of my stomach as I read and reread the message:

You are a hard person to track down, Karina. I must say, that is quite a luxurious little hideout you have found for yourself. You have had your fun, but the timer starts now. We will be in touch.

***

The grandfather clock in the main foyer rings out to signal midnight.

I have hidden in my room all day. I planned on telling Nixon I was feeling ill if he called on me for work, but as I expected, he has been locked away since our last interaction. Maggie sent me a text at teatime, telling me that she has put some leftovers in the fridge if I am looking for anything.

That woman is always looking out for me. I will never be able to thank her enough for everything that she does. She reminds me so much of my mother it hurts sometimes, but strangely enough, it is a nice pain. One that keeps the memory of my mother alive and how it felt to be loved by her.

I pull on grey jogging bottoms and the matching hoodie. After such a shitty day, there is only one thing that will do...Dessert.

I unlock my door and poke my head out, checking the coast is clear. Despite it being midnight, you just never know in this house.

I tiptoe down the hallway and the grand staircase, avoiding the squeaky floorboards as best as I can, and pad along in the darkness until I reach the kitchen.

The small light above the stove has been left on, giving the vast space a surprisingly cosy feel. It is still warm in here from a long day of cooking, and I feel the tension I have been carrying slip away for a small moment. Wasting no time, I dive into the fridge in search of the greatest remedy ever discovered.

Chocolate.

Once again, Maggie doesn't disappoint. She has wrapped some leftover chocolate cheesecake; she knows that's my favourite. Not bothering with a dish, I grab a fork and dive straight in. Standing in peaceful silence, and bathed in the warm glow from the fridge, I pile the cheesecake into my mouth.

"Mm, jeezo, Maggie. I am going to end up twenty stone if I stay here too long."

I nearly jump out of my skin as the floorboard's creek near the entrance to the kitchen. "So you do plan on leaving?" Nixon leans against the frame of the door, dressed in an outfit similar to mine. His dark eyes drop to my mouth and lock on my lips as I wipe the chocolate remains away.

"You have a habit of appearing at that doorway, like some sort of creeper," I say around my last mouthful, savouring the taste to distract me from how delicious Nixon looks wrapped in the cozy material.

"Am I a creeper if it is my house?" His raven hair falls around his eyes, and he looks like he might have just rolled out of bed. I dive back into the fridge, looking for more food, ignoring the hunger he is igniting further south than my belly.

"You're not done?" His lips twitch with amusement.

I shake my head like a toddler in a huff, which only teases a laugh out of him. I stop in my tracks, turning my head in his direction. Nixon has never looked more his age than he does right now. Dressed so casually and laughing like he hasn't a care in the world.

And what the hell is that on his face?

He has fucking dimples!

Lord, just put me out of my misery now. Why is life so unfair?

"Cake, I need more cake," I grumble more to myself than anything. I need a distraction, and I need him to leave before I do something stupid.

Again.

"Okay, hold on a minute." He slips his steady hands around my waist and lifts me effortlessly onto the countertop. "I know just what you need."

I narrow my eyes at his retreating form, wondering if he meant the innuendo, or if I just turn into a dog in heat around him. Nixon messes about in the freezer, and I try my best to peek over his shoulder. Knowing what I am doing, he laughs and blocks my view further. Which is an easy task with shoulders as broad as his.

"Close your eyes." It is worded like a demand, but there is a slight questioning tone. Like he is asking me to play and hoping I am willing to go along with whatever he has planned.

Smiling, I close my eyes and tip my chin high, to show him I am ready to follow his lead.

Nixon hums his approval for somewhere in front of me.

Something is placed on the surface at my side before the cutlery clatters in the drawer. Slowly, Nixon places his hands on my knees and pushes them wide open and steps between them.

"Fluffy socks?" He teases my bed sock over the sweatpants look.

"Hey, it's December, and this big old house gets cold."

His mouth suddenly appears at the crook of my neck, his lips tracing the shell of my ear as he whispers, "You're about to get a little colder." That smooth, deep tone wraps around me like cool silk and heat begins to pool in my centre. Having him close like this does things to my body I have never felt before. It is like every nerve ending in my body sparks and comes to life, making me hyper aware of his every move.

The brush of his thigh against mine, his large hand that is planted by my hip on the counter, close enough that his thumb teases the material of my trousers. All acts that are innocent enough, yet they set my skin ablaze.

Nixon pops the lid off whatever it is that he has pulled from the fridge. Ice cream, if I had to guess.

"Open," he demands gently and only a breath from my face, but I hesitate, which makes him chuckle mockingly. "Don't worry, I not going to shove my dick in your mouth. You are too high for that, and it is not *that* big."

He accentuates his point by pushing his hips further into my open legs, and on instinct, I squeeze my thighs closed around him. "It is pretty big," I whisper into the small space between us, my eyes still closed, but I can feel his breath on my face.

"Open up for me, little rabbit." His demand is more final this time, and my mouth falls open without hesitation, hungry for anything that he is willing to give me.

As I expect, a frozen substance hits my tongue. My mouth slams shut before any spills out over my lips, and I hum my approval as it melts. It's not ice cream, it's...

"Raspberry sorbet." Nixon's deep voice seeps into my ears, finishing my thought, and the taste explodes in my mouth. With my eyes still sealed shut, my body is on a sensory overload. "Looks like Maggie keeps us both stocked up on our favourites."

I swallow and open my mouth for another spoonful. Only this time, instead of the sorbet that slips into my mouth, it's Nixon's hot, demanding tongue. My eyes fly open, and I am met with his onyx eyes locked on mine. This close, I can see the brown flecks in his irises. Like the man himself, dark with little flashes of light if he lets you close enough to uncover.

Our eyes flutter closed together, and I moan softly at the feel of his unapologetic lips while he sucks and bites, and I run my hands through his smooth thick hair, holding him to me.

"I can taste the chocolate mixed with the raspberry on your tongue," he growls as he nips at my lips.

"More," I demand, but he pulls back, breaking contact. Getting ready to protest, my mouth quickly tilts in a grin as Nixon swallows a spoonful of sorbet before scooping another and offering it to me. "I wasn't talking about the dessert," I tease with an arched brow, but wrap my lips around the spoon, regardless.

"I know." He smirks as he watches me with a hunger the sorbet could never satisfy before dropping the spoon on the counter at my side and dragging me to the edge, pushing backwards with his chest until my back hits the cold countertop. We suck and lick the sorbet off one another slowly and thoroughly, and it is the most sensual experience of my life. Pulling back, he drags his hoodie over his head, exposing his muscular torso. The deep ridges of his abs pulling and restricting with every move.

Holy shit! I knew Nixon would have a body to rival any A-list model, but I could never have imagined this mouth-watering perfection.

And that happy trail…

Nixon's rough fingertips play with the hem of my top, pushing the fabric north until it exposes my naked breasts. His hair tickles my bare skin as he drops his head, taking my full nipple in his mouth, I groan as his cold lips circle the sensitive flesh, and admire his angular jaw and full lips as he nips and teases me until I am a panting mess, grinding against him shamelessly.

"Nixon," I beg.

"I've got you, baby. Don't worry." He reassures me without another word, slipping down his trousers and freeing his thick cock, which is already solid and leaking at the tip.

Lifting my legs, I hook my feet behind him and pull him into me with my heels digging into his butt. Unlike last night, he pushes into me slowly, savouring every inch as I squirm on the counter below him.

We both exhale together, with the relief of being joined again in the most intimate way. Like a pressure that has been building all day to an unbearable point has finally been released.

Nixon wraps his arms around my shoulders and holds me tight as he fucks into me hard and slow. His gaze bounces between my eyes and something in my chest tightens at the look I find there.

Mine.

His eyes tell me, and I have to look away before I admit things that I shouldn't. Things that would hurt us both. Instead, I lift my head and bite and suck at his neck. Desperate to leave my mark on him as he has on me. Hopeful that he won't forget me as quickly as I know he forgets all the other women who warm his bed.

Nixon grunts as he spills inside of me. His warmth sending me over the edge with him as I promise this is the last time I submit to my desires for this irresistibly gorgeous and complicated man.

Nine

Nixon

The heavens have opened and thunder rolls over the snow-topped hills in the distance.

It seems fitting. It is as though God himself is angry that my father had the audacity to ask for entry through the pearly gates.

I made sure that the details of my father's funeral were kept quiet. The staff were informed to tell anyone who enquired that we were having a small, private ceremony with close family only. Close family only, as in me and a few of the staff members who wanted to say their goodbyes.

Of course, Karina was one of them. She weeped quietly the whole way through the few short prayers that the local minister insisted on.

I picked a plot in the family graveyard far away from the place that my father had picked for himself. I don't want to walk past him if I ever decide to come and visit my mother or my grandparents. The chances of that happening are slim, but I wanted to cover all my bases. Plus, it was my second last *fuck you* to the old bastard.

The last being getting rid of this godforsaken estate and the memories that come with it.

Karina finds me in my room. I know it is her, despite having my back to the door and gazing out at the storm. Karina is the only one who would enter without permission.

"Why would you do such a thing? Why could you not just lay an old man to rest? Not just any old man, your father!" I still don't turn to face her. I am exhausted, and I fear if I show her my face right now, she will see the hurt in my eyes. Hurt because she is prioritising the feelings of a dead man who caused me a world of pain in his lifetime.

"It was less than he deserved, believe me." I rip open my shirt and throw it on the bed, the need to take a shower to wash the memory of this day away almost unbearable. "He is lucky there was even a prayer said for him and I didn't have him thrown in a hole with an unmarked headstone."

"You bastard," Karina spits into the space between us as I turn to face her, then she darts away. Running as quickly as her feet will carry her.

Without thinking, my blood now raging, I take after her. The pounding of our feet reverberates off the walls as I chase her through the house. Karina has no idea where she is headed, that much is obvious. She is merely fleeing in any direction that she can. Her feet hit the ground floor, and she flies in the direction of the game room. She swings the door behind her, but I catch it before it closes. I step into the dimly lit room, slamming it shut with as much force as I can.

Tears silently track her porcelain skin. I approach her cautiously now, reaching out gently to swipe a thumb across her cheek. "You give your tears so freely to a man who does not deserve them."

"He deserves mine."

My brows pinch, and I shake my head impatiently, urging her to explain. "Tell me why, little rabbit, I need to know."

"He saved me." Karina looks up at me with her clearwater eyes, begging me to understand, yet not to dig further, but I can't not. There are some things I need to know.

"Saved you from what, Karina?" My bare chest heaves, frustration from constantly hitting a brick wall with this woman starting to take its toll. She drops her eyes from mine and turns away, but I quickly twist her face back to mine and do something that I have never done before.

I plead.

"Give me something, baby. Please."

I wait with bated breath as she begins. "Your father knew my mother; he owed her a favour, and when she passed away, I cashed in on that favour. And here we are."

Relief floods me. Relief at what, I am not quite sure, but finally getting some form of truth out of Karina fills me with a powerful feeling that I can't explain. I grab her by the waist and carry her with her legs wrapped around my waist to the billiards table.

"And here we are," I taunt as I spread her across the blue felt on her back, her legs dangling over the edge and spread wide.

I step between her legs and tear her stockings. "Pull those panties to the side and show me that hungry little pussy."

My little rabbit obeys without having to be told twice.

"Are you wet for me, baby?" She whimpers and nods. "Show me."

Like a good girl, Karina dips two fingers into her slick little cunt, scissoring her finger inside, before pulling out and holding her hand out in offering. Her fingers glisten with her arousal, even in the low light.

I practically growl my approval. My mouth waters with the need to suck on her fingers, but I muster all my restraint.

"Lick them clean, little rabbit. I want you to taste what I do to you. I want you to taste your need for me, so that you understand why you and that little snatch of yours drives me fucking crazy."

"Nixon!" Karina sighs breathlessly.

"All in good time, baby girl. Now. Suck." Without having to tell her again, she swallows her fingers whole and sucks on them in a way that has my cock weeping.

Fuck, she looks divine. Laid out, legs spread wide, her bare pussy exposed and dripping all over the expensive blue material while going to town on her fingers like she is the best damn thing she has ever tasted.

I reach for her hand and drag it down over her body, pushing her fingers inside once again, but this time, I bring them to my mouth. I take her fingers to the base before sucking my way slowly all the way to the tip. She squirms on the table, obviously in desperate need of more. So, I tear her blouse open, her beautiful tits bouncing a little as they are freed, her nipples already rock solid and begging for attention. I pinch the hardened points and release her fingers with a pop.

With a desperate need that is reaching the point of pain, I wrap one lithe leg around my waist and hold the other up over my shoulder, before rubbing her clit in slow, deliberate circles. I sink into Karina's heat at a tortuous pace. I don't want her coming too soon.

We moan together, and I drop my mouth to hers and devour her, my whole body convulsing as I fuck her into the table. My heart pounds wildly against my rib cage, like it is trying to escape its confines to be closer to her.

"You take me so well. It's like your pussy was made for me, little rabbit. Can you feel how tight she holds on to every thrust." Karina simply nods, returning my ruthless kisses while her fingers pinch and strum over her sensitive nipples.

Fuck me, she is a wet fucking dream. Her lips swollen from my assault and her eyes dazed and blissed out. She is in another dimension right now. I know, because I am right there with her.

"Desperate." *Slap.* "Greedy." *Pinch.* "Perfect little pussy." *Thrust.*

"Nixon, please! I can't take it anymore; I need to come. Come with me, come in me."

"You want me to fill you up, little rabbit?" I taunt her in the way I know she loves.

"Oh, God, yes!" By the way she is clawing at my back, I will be disappointed if she hasn't drawn blood.

I bite down on her neck and pick up the pace, sliding a hand behind her head to stop it from hitting off the wooden frame. "You want to be so full of my come, you drip for days?"

"Yes, please!" Her hooded eyes hold mine and something that I can't put into words passes between us.

And that sends me over the edge. My vision blurs as I shoot my load into Karina bare. We groan together as we ride through our climax. She chants my name over and over and leg locks me inside of her. Warning bells should be going off, but for the first time in my life, I am too content to care.

***

"Her phone has been out of service since she arrived at the estate, sir." I recline on the chair in front of my desk and watch as my computer loads the new computer software I have coded.

Karina is avoiding me.

It has been three days since she left me in the billiards room. With one last kiss, and the excuse of having to shower, she ran off quicker than my ego was comfortable with and has been dodging me ever since.

I text or call her with tasks that I would like her to take care of, and politely, she agrees and gets to work. Communicating with me purely for work reasons and nothing more. I have tried cornering her a few times, but I am convinced she has enlisted the help of Maggie. The old woman pops out of doorways and calls her to help with the most ridiculous things. Not only that, but I also overheard her asking my cook what I was like as a young boy and if I have always been this cold and guarded.

I didn't stick around to hear the answer.

"And her laptop. What has she been looking at on there?" I could look myself. It would take me ten seconds to hack into her computer, but I don't trust myself to keep it strictly business and employer/employee laws, blah fucking blah.

"Nothing of importance, sir. No job searches."

Huffing, I throw my phone down on my desk. Maybe it is time that I accepted that I was wrong about her intentions here at Lennox House. I guess I should be happy. I am happy. But my instincts are never wrong, so I am more concerned about being wrong about this.

Was I blinded by the hate for my father, or by the unexpected pretty face at his bedside.

Perhaps both.

Anyway, I need to start focusing on the task at hand. Selling the estate.

A commotion from the foyer distracts my attention, and I strain my ears, but it is hard to make anything out through the giggling.

"*Oh, how lovely.*"

"*A secret admirer?*"

"*I have never seen anything like those before.*"

Curiosity gets the better of me, and I slip quietly out into the landing. It doesn't take long before I see what the fuss is all about.

One of the maids, I think her name is Melissa, and Maggie flutter around Karina, who is standing holding a bouquet of black roses. Yet neither of the women have realised that she is holding them like they have just taken a dump on her Dr Martens.

Who the fuck is sending her flowers and having them delivered to my front door?

I consider Ryan, but quickly dismiss the idea. He is more likely to try to whisk her away into a quiet corner to woo her privately. Not make a public display and give me a chance to outdo him.

"Well, what does the card say?" Melissa squeals with delight.

Yes, little rabbit! What does the card say?

Maggie reaches out to snatch the card, but Karina twists it out of reach. "Is a girl not allowed her secrets?"

Not in this house, sweetheart, and definitely not when it involves you.

"Spoil sport," Maggie huffs, and Karina smiles, but it doesn't reach her eyes.

I stalk along the landing above them, keeping hidden in the shadows, eyes locked on my girl, eager to get a better read on her. Something is bothering her, and I need to know what.

Black roses?

Karina doesn't strike me as the kind of girl who would be fond of something so morbid. So, whoever sent her those didn't do it because they know that they are her favourite.

Thomas, one of the boys who works the estate, appears as if right on cue, breaking up Karina's inquisition and giving me the perfect opening to reveal myself. Leaning over the carved mahogany railing, I drape my forearms over the edge, and call down to Thomas.

"Everything ready?" I address him, ignoring Karina and her flowers.

He tips his head in my direction, an excited grin spreading across his face. "Yes, sir! She is a beauty, if I do say so."

Nodding, I push off the banister and descend the grand stairs. The maid scurries away, but as I expected, Maggie stays stuck to Karina's side.

As I reach the group, I continue walking. "You're with me, Miss Campbell."

"Em, actually, Karina was helping me with a task in the kitchen, sir."

I don't stop, knowing she would give some excuse as to why Karina couldn't follow. "Tell someone who gives a shit, Maggie. There is a house full of maids to help you peel fucking potatoes. Now if you would, Miss Campbell, I do not have all day."

Thomas is quick on my heel and if Karina knows what is good for her, she will be too.

At the back of the property in the courtyard lay the old stables. My father had a new building erected away from the house around twenty years ago. When I was a young boy, I would sneak out in the middle of the night and spend hours out here. However, one day after I accidentally walked in on him fucking his secretary, he took away the thing I loved the most, making it as hard as he could for me to access them. Much to his dismay, he couldn't remove them completely. The horses are vital when it comes to hunting season.

Now that the old bastard is dead, I have had them cleaned out, and the horses moved back to where they belong. Adding a new resident.

I have had my mare from London brought up. I ride her at least once a week, and I plan to be here for the foreseeable future. I could have someone at the stable see to her; however, I thought it would be nice for her to get out and explore new terrain.

I reach for her, pulling her nose to mine, and give her a big scratch behind the ears. "Hey there, beauty. You and I are going to have some fun up here. I will make that journey worth your while, I promise."

"I thought Thomas was talking about a car." I turn my head, keeping my cheek resting against the silky coat. "Back inside, I thought Thomas was talking about a car, not a horse. She is yours?"

Karina steps closer, her fingertips twitching, and I know she is desperate to reach out and touch the magnificent Camarillo.

I nod and reach out my hand for hers. I pull her close, standing behind her so that her back in pressed against my front, and place her hand on the mare's neck. "Karina Campbell, let me introduce you to Shadowfax."

Karina pulls her head back. "I thought you said that you don't read." I smirk, satisfied that she has picked up the connection as she elaborates. "Shadowfax from Lord of the Rings? As in 'the lord of all horses' Shadowfax?"

"Are you saying she isn't worthy of such a name?" I glide my hand down my thoroughbred's smooth white coat.

"Of course not, she is absolutely breathtaking." Shadowfax whinnies under Karina's touch, happy for the compliment.

We stand there for a moment, wordlessly stroking the animal before us, and I feel the most content I have in days. Happy to have Karina back in my space. I dip my head, smelling the scent of her almond shampoo, and I know that I am in trouble.

"Do you ride?" Holding my breath for her answer, I hope she will agree to my next question, because Karina in breeches and riding boots would be a sight to behold.

"Never." Her voice quiet, but full of longing, telling me that I am in luck.

"Thomas, show Miss Campbell to the changing rooms." I step away and nudge her in the direction of the outhouse. "There will be something in there that fits you. Don't be long."

Thomas saddles up Valkyrie. He says she is an old, unflappable thing who has always been calm and reliable. In other words, the perfect candidate for Karina's first ride.

I saddle up on Shadowfax, my all-black outfit in complete contrast to her white coat, and I stroke her mane with my gloved hands.

"You will love it here, girl, just wait until you see the glen on the other side of the forest."

Shadowfax kicks at the gravel under her feet while Thomas makes the finishing touches to Valkyrie.

I look at my watch and roll my eyes. "Karina, darling, we really haven't got all day. We want to make it home before sundown."

"Coming, coming." My sassy little redhead comes striding from the outhouse, dressed in the tightest white jodhpurs and looking every inch the lady of the manor. Her hips sway like a model who has just stepped off a vogue shoot set in the countryside, making my mouth dry instantly at the sight of her.

Thomas holds Valkyrie in place as Karina uses the mounting block he has brought out for her.

"That's right, Miss Campbell, now hold on to the reins and the saddle and slip your foot in the stirrup." Karina bends at the waist, giving us both a front-row view of her spandex covered arse. Thomas tilts his head and shifts on his feet. He is gawking at her, and I don't like it. Not one bit.

I pull on my reins, which causes Shadowfax to head butt Thomas on the shoulder. He snaps his head in my direction and is met with my burning glare. The leather of the reins creaks under my tight grip as I strangle the strap and arch my brow at him, daring him to look at her again and see what happens.

Using more subtlety than me, he nods his head and gets back to the task at hand, but keeping his eyes firmly locked on her face now. Thomas encourages Karina, like a good stable hand should. "Excellent, now swing your leg over and slip it into the stirrup."

We lock eyes as we buckle our helmets. "Take it easy on me." Karina grins, her face radiant with obvious excitement.

"Just be a good girl and do as you are told. As I remember, you follow instructions quite well."

Karina takes to it like natural, and despite Valkyries age, she keeps up well with the pace Shadowfax and I have set. We gallop through the woods, inhaling lungfuls of cold fresh air as we fly past the towering Rowan trees and green pines.

The trees disappear, and we ride out onto the open glen. The snow on the lower ground has mostly melted, but the mountains stand proudly behind, dusted in white ice and snow at their peaks.

I am thankful for the riding gloves, as the cold bite in the air chases us, nipping at our tales as we explore the wild terrain. Our breath and the breath of the horses' fogs in the air before us. Waterfalls have frozen on the hills and a falcon makes a swoop to the ground before soaring back into the air with his dinner for the evening. Karina pants at my side, a huge smile engulfing her rosy face as she takes in the beauty surrounding us.

"This is all part of the Lennox estate?" she asks, staring into the distance. I nod without glancing at the view, my eyes locked on her. She is more beautiful than the dramatic backdrop could ever be.

Karina turns, of course, as I answered her without words. Tipping her chin up in question, I nod once more.

"What was your life like before you came here?" Karina opens her mouth to answer, but I cut her off. "Tell me something that I won't find on your resume."

She pulls on Valkyrie's reins and circles me. I watch her every move with fascination. "Hard. Nothing like your life, I am sure."

I narrow my eyes, swallowing the urge to tear into her with insults. I am determined not to ruin our afternoon with my natural instincts and dazzling ability at being an arsehole. It isn't Karina's fault she doesn't know what, when on inside our home all those years ago, very few people do. "Just because we had money doesn't mean my life did not have its challenges."

"Yes, I do not doubt it. Though, I am sure that our struggles were not the same." She strokes Valkyrie's mane absently, and I tell myself that she didn't mean for that to sound as condescending as it did.

"Tell me." I squeeze Shadowfax with my knees, encouraging her to take me closer to the infuriating woman who has made herself the object of all my current desires, and quite frankly, every fucking waking thought.

"You don't need to know my heart, Nixon."

"What if I want to?"

"You don't. It is just your natural instincts to conquer everything that dares to step on to your radar and not immediately submit to your will."

I think about her words. A little bit shocked that she would admit that out loud, no one has ever spoken to me as frankly as my little rabbit does, and I adore her for it. That is when I realise that she couldn't be more wrong. Perhaps it started that way. A stranger was in my home, claiming that she had a right to be there and there was nothing that I could do about it. But things have changed. Now she has wormed her way under my skin and has made it her mission to eat me alive from the inside out. And the most shocking part is, I want her to fucking devour me. I want to tell her to have it all, to not even leave the bones when she is done with me. But then I remember myself and pull my head out of the goddamn clouds. Karina Campbell will never see me as anything more. Who could ever love the cold-hearted heir of Lennoxshire? Best to not even try. That is how I have always liked it. I don't let people close. People are problems and I have enough of my own.

"Come, we're heading back. Looks like a storm is rolling in over the mountains." I squeeze my legs and guide Shadowfax in the direction of the house, not caring this time if Karina follows or not.

Arriving back home, we dismount in silence, our shoes clicking against the cobbled stones, all the jovial and teasing behaviour from earlier long gone.

"I am sure Maggie will be waiting for you in the kitchen." My glare and commanding tone ruffle her feathers even more, and she purses her lips as she stomps off in the old woman's direction.

That's right, little rabbit, spend as long as you want moaning about me in there to anyone who will listen. You are only lying to yourself.

Now it is time for me to find out a little bit of truth.

Taking the steps two at a time, I head straight for Karina's room. Just as I thought, Maggie has had the morbid bouquet sat pride of place in front of the bay window. I pull the card out of its clip and study the matching black envelope, front and back. No sign of where these flowers were ordered from.

Slowly slipping the card out, making sure not to show any sign of disruption, I study the embossed text.

The clock is ticking...

I gently flip the card in my fingers, making sure that I have not missed anything. My eyes narrow in frustration.

What the fuck does that mean?

It would seem that I have been right about my little rabbit all along. She has secrets, and I intend on dragging them out of her. If she is here to interfere with the estate in any way before I am through with my own savage plans, then Karina is in for a rude awakening.

Ten

Karina

Nixon Lennox infuriates me like no one else ever has, and the fact that I give him the power over my emotions by letting him affect me in such an all-consuming way merely serves to frustrate me further.

He thinks that he can demand information from me, yet refuses to give any in return. Nixon is a closed book, giving away only the information that is strategic to his cause at that given time.

How dare he!

"Dear, I think it is best that you call it a night." Maggie slides the bread knife from beneath my fingers. "I will have this sent up to up to you. Now go and retire for the evening."

I wrap my arms around her, breathing in her comforting scent and mumbling words of gratitude. Maggie will never know how much I appreciate every small way that she looks out for me, and it breaks my heart that I won't be able to come back and visit her after I leave this place.

I am combing my hair when heavy and urgent raps rattle the door. My stomach dips, and I scold my instincts for the reaction. Despite everything and the fact that I am mad with him beyond belief, I hope that it is Nixon that has come to find me.

"Karina, let me in." My eyes squeeze closed in relief. Just the sound of his deep, smooth voice is enough to steal the air from my lungs and rid me of all rational thoughts.

Cautiously, I step towards the door and in the direction of the man who drives me crazy with a confusion that, before Nixon arrived at Lennox House, I had been fortunate enough to never experience.

Love.

As quick as the insane thought flashes in my brain, I dismiss it. Not because Nixon is unlovable, but it is the opposite. I can see myself falling into Nixon irrevocably and never coming back. Not in one piece, anyway. Nixon is magnetic and fascinating and frustrating but goddamnit, I want him to be mine.

I don't remember opening the door, my body acting on want and instinct. Nixon now stands a breath away from me like he wants to reach out to touch me, but not before what he came here to say. I find myself anticipating his next words like the drop of a rollercoaster after a slow climb to the peak. Only this suspense has been keeping me impatient for his truth since the moment I laid my eyes on his weeks ago.

"Alexander Lennox was my father in title only. For as long as I can remember, he disciplined me with beatings, emotional and mental abuse, and finally when my mother died, he had me sent away, because even the sight of me would set him off in one of his vile and violent moods that would last for days on end. He decided it would be better for him to have someone else do the hard work of raising me. Alexander did everything in his power to demean me and make it known that he thought I was unworthy of being his sole heir. I cannot remember when I realised that I didn't want to continue his legacy, that the best way of punishing a narcissist like my father was to erase his memory and decimate all that he worked for. As his legacy was all that he ever cared about."

I'm floored, like someone has taken a sledgehammer to my gut, and then put me in a chokehold. Nixon delivers these heartbreaking truths with a cold mask of indifference. The only hint that his admissions affect him is the quick rise and fall of his panting chest. His hands are dug deep into the pockets of his black slacks to hide his balled fists, I am sure of it.

I can't take it any longer. I pounce on him, wrapping my legs around his waist, and dragging both hands around the back of his head until I have fists full of his inky hair. Nixon catches me effortlessly, barely taking a step back to catch his balance. Our mouths find each other like two magnets, and I don't ask for permission as I slip my tongue over his. I can taste the mint in his breath, and the wild and untamed fragrance from our ride outside still lingers on him.

My thighs squeeze him in appreciation, and he nips at my bottom lip in return. His hot and enticing mouth, which is a stark contrast to his cold skin, expertly teases me, caressing my tongue and sucking on my lips. It isn't long until I am grinding my centre shamelessly against his rock-hard abs. Silently begging him to give us what we both crave.

I loosen my legs, and Nixon lets me slide down his body, my feet gently hitting the floor as I make quick work of his belt and zipper. I guide him backwards until his knees hit the soft mattress, and I have pulled him free of his slacks before his butt has hit my plush bedcovers.

"Little rabbit," Nixon growls, and I'm not sure if even he knows if it is in warning or appreciation. But I don't give either of us time to think.

We need this. This connection that is undeniable, and I feel like I am going fucking crazy every second of the day because all I want is to have him near me, on me, *in* me. Physically and emotionally.

God, what is happening to me?

No, not right now. Right now, I am going to have my man, and I am going to take him any way that I want him. I can worry about the rest when the sun rises tomorrow.

Back arched and propped on my knees, I look up at Nixon sitting on my bed with his legs spread wide. Even with his pants down and his thick length heavy in both of my fists, he still manages to look like a proud prince. But then I see it, and it takes my last breath from my lungs. The look of sheer awe and admiration in his hooded eyes.

I need no further encouragement. I lick his length firmly from base to tip, getting him as wet as possible, determined to please him even half as much as he pleases me. Nixon hisses with frustrated pleasure every time I skim past his tip. Precome is gathering there, and my mouth waters uncontrollably with the need to taste him.

"Fuck, baby, you're killing me!" He scoops my hair up expertly with both hands, assuring his view is unobscured. His voice rough and scratchy, like he has run a marathon, and I take that as my cue to put us both out of our misery.

On the next upwards sweep of my tongue, I catch the swollen head of his cock, enclosing it completely in my mouth and swirling my tongue around the tip. We moan in unison as I lick every salty drop of precome and revel in the sensory overload that comes from being intimate with Nixon like this. Every time is so intense, I wonder if I can handle it, yet it is never nearly enough, and I am left, like an addict, craving more with embarrassing desperation.

And I know Nixon feels the same way.

I dip my head and take him as far down my throat as possible, swallowing as best as I can around his thick length. From the flex of his muscular thighs, it is obvious that Nixon is battling with his need to take control.

"Can I?" he shocks me by asking, but with his monstrous cock stretching my throat, I can only nod my head a fraction as a reply.

Nixon slides himself to the back of my throat, testing my limits, and I squeeze his thighs, letting him know without words that I am good as I moan around his length.

A knock at the door sounds, and my eyes fly to his. My stomach flips at the dark delight that I find there. I try to pull back, to free myself from his cock, but as I feared, he holds me steady.

"Karina, I have your supper. Maggie sent me up." My worst nightmare comes to life as Ryan calls from the other side of the door, only a few meters away.

Nixon dips his head towards me. "Go on, little rabbit, tell him you're busy." His dark and sinful voice taunts me in a way that makes me slick between my thighs, and he accentuates his command with a small thrust.

Ryan knocks once again, calling my name before trying the handle. Everything slows down as from my side, I see the door swing open in slow motion. Ryan takes in the scene before him, and I feel my face flush in shame.

"Fuck, sorry-" Ryan's words catch in his throat as realisation of what is happening and who I am doing it with sets in.

I can't bear to look in his direction, so I keep my gaze firmly on Nixon, and that is when I witness his eyes flare with sadistic satisfaction.

"You can tell Maggie that Karina found something else to satisfy her cravings." Nixon strokes my hair like I am his favourite pet before sliding my mouth down his length further.

God strike me down, but I get slicker between my legs. I am positive my panties are soaked now, and if I stood up, both men would see a wet patch.

Fuck! More wetness pools at that thought, and with horror, I realise that I must have some sort of degradation or humiliation kink? Or does this make me a voyeur?

I don't know. All I know is that any minute now, I might start humping Nixon's leather shoes just to get some sort of relief from the need building in my core.

Saliva spills from the corners of my mouth. I watch as Nixon's eyes drop to my hardened nipples poking shamelessly through my top, desperately seeking attention, and the rocking motion of my hips as I try and fail to get some friction against my aching clit.

I am so obviously turned on by the whole sordid affair, and I don't even care who knows it. I would slip my fingers inside my dripping pussy if I thought that Nixon would allow it, but I know that the orgasm that he will give me for this will be better than anything I would ever be able to do to myself.

"What do you say, baby? Will we let him stay and watch?" Nixon tilts his head in Ryan's direction, daring him to make a move.

Nixon scoffs, and with his dick still stuffed down my throat and his grip on my hair, he twists my head in the direction of the door. The tops of Ryan's sharp cheekbones are tinged pink in the way that I know they do when he is turned on, and my eyes drop to the noticeable bulge in his trousers.

We had sex, but I never sucked Ryan off, and I see the jealousy a blaze in his eyes. Somehow, I know, though, it has nothing to do with me and more to do with some sort of fucked-up alpha competition between the two men.

However, despite all of this, he is turned on.

Without another word, Ryan leaves. Followed by Nixon's demonic laughter as he slips himself out of my mouth and lifts me easily onto his lap. He shreds the soaked silk material of my sleep shorts and lowers me onto his thick cock without pause. My groan is delight mixed with relief as he stretches me to capacity in the most delicious way. My inner walls squeeze him in appreciation as I ride him slowly, savouring every inch of him.

"You are one sick bastard, Nixon Lennox." I grab him by the throat to anchor myself as I ferally grind my hips.

"Don't feel too sorry for him." With one sharp tug, Nixon frees my breasts and nips at them with his teeth and lips. "He has been fucking Melissa for weeks now. I am sure he is on his way to find her as we speak to rid him of his *little* problem."

I don't miss his insult at Ryan's expense, but I can't even find it in myself to defend him as I ride my way to the gates of paradise on the lap of the mortal god beneath me.

"You are going to come all over my cock, and then I am going to come down that pretty little throat." His filthy words send me over the edge, and I groan his name over and over as waves of unworldly pleasure douse my body.

Instead of dropping me back to my knees, Nixon flips us on the bed and crawls up my body. He lifts my head and slips his cock, slick with my orgasm, back between my lips. "Hmm, that's my good girl," he praises and strokes my hair once again, encouraging me as I choke around his fat cock. As it pulses out ropes of salty come, I swallow every last drop as best as I can. "You take me so well. It's like you were made for me, my little rabbit."

I bask in his adoration, all thoughts and worries of the outside world firmly locked away for the night. That is, until Nixon finds the shell of my ear, and through the cloud of impending slumber, serves me a word of warning like some fucked-up villainous Disney prince. "I am going to find out what it is that is holding you back from giving yourself to me completely, Karina, and I am going to obliterate it."

I have spent the last week moving around the house, trying to be as invisible as possible. Helping with the Christmas trees, because yes, there are more Christmas trees around this enormous house than I can count, and hanging all manner of decorations on every fireplace and window in sight. Nixon has cornered me a handful of times, dragging me into the nearest room to ravage my mouth while he wraps my legs around his waist and my hair around his fist. Nixon has sex like he lives his life. Intensely, with a sole focus on his end game. Nothing can distract him from getting what he wants, and I can't say that I am complaining when the thing he wants is me.

I am left as nothing more than a puddle of the floor, with wobbly legs and a frantic heart rate.

What are you hiding from me, little rabbit? Are the words he whispered against my gasping open mouth as he thrust into me relentlessly last night.

I can't tell him. He will never understand, and if he ever finds out, there will be no going back for us. I just hope that I am long gone before he discovers my truth.

***

Another day spent hiding in my room. I feel like a terrible storm is surging in my direction, and I am powerless to stop it, no matter how deep I try to bury my head in the sand.

I power up my laptop with the intention of researching visas and, almost instantly, a message pops up on the screen.

The boy won't save you.

I slam the computer closed and throw it across the bed. I knew he wouldn't leave me alone. I was never going to be left to get on with my life without my mother. I wipe my sweaty hands down my jeans frantically, trying to plan my next move.

I need to get out of here.

Nixon is out visiting a handful of farmers who live on the estate and shouldn't be home till late. The time has come.

I can't do this anymore. The longer that I remain at Lennox House, the more danger I am putting people in. I stare longingly at the small Christmas tree that Maggie insisted I put in my room. It is very minimal, a little thing with silver tinsel and wrapped in twinkling crystal lights.

I wish with all my heart that I could stay, but they will come for me eventually. I know that much.

I throw my belongings into my bag, not bothering to take care or put things in any sort of order. I don't even know where I will go from here; I just know I need to be gone before Nixon returns.

"Where do you think you are running off to, little rabbit?" I spin on my heel, my throat sinking into my gut at the sound of his rough, threatening voice, and God help me, my thighs squeeze of their own accord.

In my panic, I didn't hear him opening the bedroom door. He stands, as he has so many times before, leaning a shoulder on the doorframe. He has his head dropped and is inspecting his hands and shirt cuffs like he cannot bear to look at me.

"Running off ahead of schedule, are you not?" A nasty smirk pulls at his full lips, doing a poor job of covering his hurt.

"I-I need... I can't stay here any longer. Please, Nixon, please understand and don't ask me any questions." He lifts his eyes and looks at me through fallen strands of inky black hair, his eyes narrowed, like he doesn't trust a move that I make yet has no intention of letting me walk out the door. "It is for the best if I just leave now. I am sorry for insisting that I stay longer. You were right. I don't belong here, and it is time that I left. Consider the contract null and void."

I need to leave; I can't have him getting hurt because of me. My troubles will follow me, so if I am gone and away from here, that means that danger will be far away from Nixon and everyone that I care about at Lennox House.

"Hmm, if you say so." Nixon pushes off the door frame and stalks towards me. His gate, sure and steady, and as deadly as a viper with a *little rabbit* in its sights.

The nickname has never been so fitting. Or maybe it always has been, and I have just never realised it until now. Blind to reality, as I always thought that I had the upper hand-until this very moment.

On instinct, I open my mouth to scream, waiting for him to pounce. But Nixon is too fast. He lunges for me and wraps a hand around my throat. "No one is here to hear you scream, Karina. I sent them all to the Christmas party out at the McMillan Inn. I thought we would have the whole house to ourselves tonight, that you wouldn't need to worry about anyone hearing you *give in* to someone who you insist that you loathe so much." His hand tightens, and his eyes darken, until there is no trace of the warm chocolate colour that I love so much, leaving two black glistening stones of onyx in their place.

"Instead, I come home to you making a midnight dash. So what? You were just planning on leaving and not saying goodbye. To anyone? Why can you not just tell me what I want to know and admit that you belong here, with me!"

I gasp for breath in his grip, but the panic I had been feeling before has dissipated. If this is the end, then so be it. No more running, no more hiding. "Nixon, I-"

Just as I grip onto his wrist and pull myself closer to him, the lights go out, cloaking us in immediate darkness.

"What the fuck?" Nixon whispers, more to himself than me.

He drops my neck and grabs my hand, pulling me out of my bedroom and in the direction of his office.

As we run down the hallway, there is banging and yelling echoing throughout the hall from the outside.

"Whoever it is, they aren't inside yet. The security I put in place will keep them out until the police arrive." Nixon tries to reassure me, and I can tell that he isn't overly worried judging by the calmness in his voice. But I know exactly who is outside, and I know it will not take them long to break through Nixon's security...if they haven't already.

Nixon closes and locks the door to his office, his hold on my hand steady and unrelenting as he guides me behind him to one of the desks. His fingers fly across the keyboard and the security cameras appear on the screen, one by one. All the cameras inside the house show no sign of disturbance, and my heart slows a fraction.

Maybe Nixon is right, maybe his security system will keep them out. A few clicks and the cameras from outside flash on the screen. And there, just as I knew they would be, are standing masked men. Dressed in all black, with their faces hidden behind neon masks. The crossed-out eyes and stitched-up mouths glow in the darkness of the night in an array of colours, but I know exactly who is who.

The red mask at the main entrance tilts his creepy face to the side and knocks on the camera before giving a slow wave. Blue, purple and green at the back of the house and at the entry to the kitchen stand with their arms and legs crossed at the ankles, looking like they have no care in the world.

Nixon doesn't realise that those men outside are more than mere cat burglars. Reenforced windows, doors and keypad entries will not deter them. There is a load bang from the rear of the house, and I can't hold back the yelp that slips from my throat. Nixon notices the uncontrollable tremor that has taken hold of my body and tucks me under his arm as his fingers fly across the keyboard.

He curses under his breath, and I can do nothing more than look up at him expectantly.

"My system is cut off from the outside. I can only access my internal system." His brows are drawn in confusion, and I am sure Nixon is clueless as to how these men have gotten past his high-tech security system. Especially one that he has designed himself.

Nixon makes quick work, and the monitors around the room shut down. No doubt he is securing the data he has saved in them.

We stand before the last screen that he has left powered up and watch the men connect their own laptop to the security panel at the staff entry at the back of the house.

I know it will not be much longer before they get inside.

"Listen carefully to me, Karina, in my father's room at the back of the closet, there is a panic room." He walks to the fireplace and pulls an iron poker from the grate. Nixon places it in the palm of my hand before tightly wrapping my fingers around the handle. "You are going to run there as quickly and as quietly as you can before they get inside. I will stay here and cause a distraction if I need to."

"Nixon, listen to me, please..."

"And you will not stop until you get there, Karina. No matter what you hear." The command in his voice is clear that he is not going to negotiate with me on this. He understands now that it is not a case of *if* but *when* they get inside. Silent tears slip down my cheeks, because my selfless and heartbreakingly devastating dark prince doesn't realise that I am the one who brought these wolves to his door. I will not let him deal with the consequences of my shitty circumstances.

"Nixon!"

"Please, Karina!" His eyes are wild with fear for me, and I can't understand what I have done to deserve the devotion of this man.

"I can't leave you here! They are here for me," I yell my confession at him, louder than I intend. It is not Nixon's fault we are in this situation, after all.

He points at the screen. "This is what you have been hiding from me?"

I don't answer him. I can't

"If you needed help, why the fuck did you not come to me, Karina? I thought the worst of you, and you let me. You didn't need to hide your problems from me, baby. Don't you know I would do anything that you asked of me. Give you anything that you needed? I am here for you, whatever it takes."

Nixon grabs my face with both hands and desperately slams his mouth into mine. My tears fall more freely now, at the helplessness of our situation and for the future that I might have had with this beautiful man if it wasn't for my inability to shake my fucked-up past.

There is more pounding and cracking from outside that drags us right back to reality, followed by hysterical, manic laughter.

"I can't have you out here, unprotected, when they get inside. Now go!" Nixon grabs my hand and drags me to the foot of the stairs that lead to his father's room. With my eyes blurred with tears, I take the steps two at a time, with no intention of going to the panic room like Nixon has insisted, but to find weapons to help him fight our intruders instead.

I feel his dark eyes on my back as he watches me from below. I am about to hit the first floor, but instead of the landing, a dark figure in the red mask slips silently around the corner, and I land right in his waiting arms.

"Got ye," a familiarly lifeless voice seeps into my ear.

Nixon calls for me, but before he can take a step in my direction, the rest of the men crowd him. He throws his fist at one and knocks another over with an elbow to the face, but he is outnumbered, and it doesn't take long before they kick him to his knees. They grip him by the hair and make him watch as red mask wraps his arms around my torso, capturing my trembling limbs at my sides in a vice like grip.

"Get your hands off her, you filthy bastard!" Nixon snarls like a wild bear caught in a snare trap.

Green mask kicks him in the gut, and Nixon takes the blow silently. I, however, scream as though I was the one who was hit. "Or you will do what, you wee prick? I may not have the education that you have, but I am pretty sure there are more of us than there are of you."

They all laugh as they take it in turns to kick and punch Nixon, who is still on his knees but now has his hands cable tied behind his back.

Red mask drags me downstairs, and despite taking a beating, Nixon's eyes track his every movement. "How about we get better reacquainted, Karina?" he announces loud enough for Nixon to hear above the thumps against his flesh.

At the obvious threat towards me, Nixon tries to push to his feet once again, but his legs are quickly swept from beneath him.

"Enough!" Red shouts, and as I knew they would, the rest of the men stop immediately. "Let's take this someplace more comfortable, shall we?"

He nods in the direction of the library, and I realise with dread that they have been watching us for some time. They clearly know the entire layout of the estate.

I knew I wasn't crazy when I felt eyes on me that day in the gardens.

My chest constricts painfully as I watch them drag a fighting Nixon into his office and bind his ankles to the legs of one of the chairs.

The men push me between one another, back and forth, until I am dizzy with no sense of direction. "Please," I beg. For what, I am not sure.

"Enough," Nixon's growl silences the room as they all watch and wait to see how their leader is going to respond to the threat.

"My men have worked hard to get here. Surely, they are allowed to enjoy the spoils of their victory?" Red swipes my hair off my shoulders as his creepy stitched-out eyes remain fixated on Nixon.

My heart cracks down the middle, watching helplessly as Nixon struggles against his binds, throwing all sense of self-preservation out of the window. "Over my dead fucking body."

Red tuts and chuckles humourlessly. "Now that can be arranged." He unsheathes a knife and scrapes it threateningly across Nixon's neck. His face quickly morphs to anger when he sees no fear in Nixon's defiant eyes.

I gulp. If I know our intruders like I think I do, they are going to up the ante. Nixon Lennox, the 16th Earl of Lennoxshire, is everything they have been raised to despise and will use any means necessary to hit him where it hurts. But he doesn't know Nixon and there is nothing that you can do to him physically that will make him crumble and bow at your feet. The abuse that he survived as a child has built an impenetrable shield around him and created the opposite of the typical, weak silver-spooned nobleman that Red assumes he will be.

He swings the blade in my direction. "Her."

The group jeers as both of my arms are outstretched on either side by two masked men, the lights dim, and the neon lights cast a sinister glow around the room like some fucked-up funhouse nightmare.

Red swaggers in my direction, and in one lightning-fast motion, swipes his blade down my front. My top splits down the middle, the fabric falling open and the sharp metal leaving a shallow slice down my sternum in its wake.

The men cheer once again like a pack of rabid dogs, and the two holding my arms tighten their grip as I try feebly to break free.

"We want that show now, don't we, lads? So who is it going to be?"

"You are all dead men." Nixon thrashes wildly in the chair he is strapped to, his neck bulging so ferociously I can see every vein from here.

"Looks like we have a volunteer, lads," Red taunts, and I whimper as a third man at my back strips me of my trousers. The men let me go and push me in the direction of Nixon.

His body tries to reach for me as I trip over my shaking limbs, but it is useless, as he is incapacitated.

"Fuck him and make it good, or one of the boys will show your little boyfriend here how a real man shags his whore."

Red brings his blade back to Nixon's neck when he senses my hesitation and reality hits me like a poisoned dagger to the heart.

I have no choice. Something terrible is going to happen here tonight, but this is the least evil of any of the possible options. I fall to my knees at Nixon's feet and look up into his dark, impenetrable eyes. He shakes his head once, telling me wordlessly not to do this, but we both know that there is no other way out of this. With shaky hands, I unzip his slacks and slip my hands inside. Unsurprisingly, Nixon isn't hard. Not even a little, so I pull him out and slide him into my mouth. Even soft, it doesn't fit in its entirety, and I close my eyes and pretend that we are anywhere else but here.

The men hoot and holler, and I do all that I can to ignore the humiliation that slithers up my spine like a poisonous serpent. Unlike last time, I am not getting off from being watched. I lift my chin and lock eyes with the true victim in all of this. Nixon's jaw flexes, and I know he is doing all that he can to ignore our unwanted spectators.

With my best efforts, it's not long until Nixon is hard and ready, and I stand on weak legs, selfishly wishing that Nixon wasn't bound and could take control like he does so well. But he is, and it is down to me to make this convincing enough to save the life of the man who would have saved mine, if I had just given him the chance.

Eleven

Nixon

"Don't worry, baby. Eyes on me. It is just you and me."

The men circle around us, perched on computer desks or leaning against bookshelves. We are utterly surrounded.

Karina weeps softly into my shoulder as she sinks herself down my length. I twist my head and kiss the side of her throat as sneers and insults echo around us.

"Look at her, she's cock hungry."

"Little slut."

"Bet her snug little cunt tastes delicious."

"Look at those tits jiggle."

Their barbs are thrown at her like daggers, and I see her face every time she takes a hit. It breaks me that I can't wrap my arms around her and shield her from their lecherous eyes or make this easier for her in anyway.

"Bite my shoulder if it helps," I whisper into her ear as I nestle my nose under her hair and kiss the shell of her ear the way that she likes, doing everything that I can to distract her from this hell.

She shakes her head and adjusts herself on my lap, cupping my jaw in her hands and kissing me slowly at first, but then with a passionate urgency I haven't felt from her before. Her lips taste of her salty tears, and I lick them clean as best as I can as she rides me now like these assholes aren't watching.

"Bounce on him," Purple growls, who was standing in the back before but has now moved closer and is rubbing the crotch of his trousers. "Bounce on his cock like the hungry little cum slut you are."

Karina cries softly against me as laughter ripples around the room at the scumbags' words. I want to tell him to shut the fuck up, but I channel all of my focus and energy on my girl.

"You're doing so well, baby. Just look at me." I nudge her face with my nose. "Open your eyes and look at me. Forget them. It is just me and my little rabbit, taking my cock like the good girl she is."

I thrust my hips up into her, causing her to fall back a little, just like I wanted, so that I can dip my head and capture one of her nipples. Karina moans my name, and like the asshole that I am, even in this fucked-up situation, my chest puffs a little at the knowledge that it is my name that she is panting in front of this bunch of bastards.

My thrusts become relentless, driving up into her, helping her along, so that we can get this over and done with. Sensing my urgency, Karina digs her fingers into my shoulders and grinds down into me, and it doesn't take long before I am emptying myself inside of her as her pussy spasms around me, squeezing out every last drop.

"It's almost over," she mumbles against my lips, and I reassure her with everything that I have in return.

"Yeah, baby. This will all be over soon, don't worry."

"What a great show." The asshole in the green mask steps forward, clapping his hands and purrs against my girl's bare back. "I think that I will have my shot now."

He drags Karina off me, kicking and screaming, and I pull with every fucking thing that I have to free myself. My open slacks stretch to their limit against my straining muscles, as I try but fail to stand up.

Blue mask delivers a right hook to my jaw, but I can't feel a thing because I am forced to watch on helplessly as Green straddles a completely naked and sobbing Karina who is calling my name over and over for help.

No, no, no!

"Touch a fucking hair on her head, and I swear to God, you will pay." I am practically foaming at the mouth, desperately trying to reach my girl, thrashing so violently, my chair rocks on two legs and I am caught mid-air from behind before I crash onto my face.

"You want to save your girl?" Red mask, who I have gathered is the leader, speaks from my right-hand side.

"Give us the access code to the Salvadore account, or every guy in this room will have a shot at your whore."

Access into the Salvadore system? That is what they wanted all along?

The Salvadores are one of the biggest crime families in the US, and it took me a long time to gain their trust enough for them to do business with me. I know the repercussions if I do this.

They will kill me for it, but that pales into complete and utter insignificance, when Karina is before me in immediate danger. I will do anything to get her out of this. Even if it means my certain demise when we get out of here.

I don't even hesitate. "The screen behind you." Red mask nods at Blue to follow my instruction. "23n114#." I give him the code to access the computer, and then talk him through the system until they get the information they want.

"Excellent, it has been a pleasure doing business with you." The men begin to clear out. But my eyes remain locked on the fucker who is still straddling my girl. "Everyone out, boats back to the checkpoint and we will regroup there."

The loch, that's how they approached undetected. They didn't try to get through the gate.

"Any problems, you know the drill." He continues talking while he grabs Green's arm and hauls him to his feet. "You too, Karina. Someone get some clothes for my baby sister."

What. The. Fuck?

My brain is hazy, and I blink my eyes as I watch Red reach out a hand and pull Karina off the floor before handing her a mismatched t-shirt and jumper collected off the others.

I can do nothing more that stare in silence at the scene before me. Karina slips her clothes on and gathers with the rest of them.

Green appears at my side, and I can't even make a move to defend myself. "Aw, you actually thought she had feelings for you. Not that one right there. That little firecracker is incapable of loving anyone. If I had to guess, that part of her died along with her useless mother." I want to tell him to shut the fuck up, but I can't deny what I am seeing before my eyes and, quite frankly, I am confused to fuck. "I guess it is all good for us, though. Makes her one hell of a solider."

Karina approaches me, stopping just out of reach. "You should have just let me leave when I asked, Nixon."

I can't even find it in myself to look at her. The treachery tearing me up and setting me ablaze from the inside out.

"This hurts more than it should," I mutter, to myself but from the pained look on her face, she heard. "You better run, little rabbit, and never come back. I will make you pay for this one way or another, make no mistake of that."

Karina cups my jaw, twists my face and looks at me with pure genuinity. "I am counting on it."

And with that, she turns and leaves with the masked men, leaving me with nothing but rage, disappointment and a burning hunger for revenge.

Twelve

Karina

It hurts.

It is like someone has ripped my heart out through my ribcage with their bare hands and thrown it in the shredder.

My whole-body aches and my head is a mess. I can't quite be sure how I manage to keep up with the guys.

We run down past the old bridge to the three boats that are docked at the jetty. And my stepbrother, Rafa, rips off his red mask and passes me a handgun. "It wouldn't have come to this if you had just stolen the codes yourself like we asked. This is all on you baby sis."

"You don't realise what you have just done. Nixon won't stop until he finds us."

Rafa stops and faces the house before casting me a menacing glare. "So you are saying that I should go back inside and kill him? Maybe you are more like us than I thought."

Dread fills me, and I panic. "N-no, we need to leave. We can't be sure that he hasn't broken free, and the police could show up any minute."

He considers it for a moment longer than I am comfortable with before nodding and dragging me in the direction of the boats. "The Salvadores will do that job for us anyway. He won't last forty-eight hours. Lennox won't be coming after anyone."

My gut churns at the thought of Nixon being left to the wrath of the Salvadores, as they don't take betrayal lightly. Five of us in total, we split off into the boats, and that is when I notice my father, the head of the McCloy mob, sitting at the helm of the speed boat my stepbrother and I boarded. Gavin McCloy never married my mother, that is why I go by my mum's maiden name and not my fathers. My mum spent her entire life keeping me out of the violent grasp of my father and his organisation, but when she passed, he somehow found me. That is why, after years of being used as a pawn in his crimes, I sought refuge with Alexander Lennox. I naively thought a man as powerful has him could keep me off the radar, but it didn't take my father long to find me and tell me of his plans and my critical part in them. I wanted to run before I was forced to carry out their plans, but then Nixon Lennox happened, and I couldn't bring myself to betray him or to leave him.

Rafa is right, this is all on me. Nixon's blood will be on my hands.

"Is it done?" he asks my stepbrother without sparing me a glance.

Rafa nods at our father, my father by blood and his by marriage, pulls his hand gun from his waistband and drops it on the bench and quickly retrieves his laptop. "Drive us back to the checkpoint, Karina."

The other boats kick-start their engines, and I take one last look at the house. Regret tastes bitter on the tip of my tongue. Rafa pulls out his phone, and I think about everything that Nixon has given up for me. Nixon was knowingly giving his life for mine. He knows that there is no way the Salvadores won't come for their revenge.

Without thinking my plan all the way through, I grab Rafa's semi-automatic and fire it at the accompanying boats as they flee the dock. Taking down the men in each boat easily. Rafa lunges for me, smacking me across the face and tearing the gun from my grip.

"You fucking bitch, what do you think you are doing?"

Without replying, I throw myself at him, taking us both to the floor. I knee him in the balls with everything that I have before Rafa throws a punch to my rib cage. In return, I head butt him in the nose, but he catches me and locks me in a chokehold.

"Enough!" our father yells from behind. He thinks we are just squabbling like we did as kids, but I am ready to kill these motherfuckers. My stepbrother drags me across the floor by his hold around my neck.

"She needs to go, Dad; she is a liability now." To my horror, but not taking me by surprise, our father nods, giving his son by choice the green light.

My vision blurs as his hold gets tighter, but I manage to move us closer and closer to the handgun. My fingertips kiss the handle, but the darkness is fogging my vision, and my hearing is muffled.

Then Nixon's heartbroken face flashes in my mind, giving me the strength to make one last stretch for the weapon. I can't let him take the fall for me. Even if it is the last thing that I do, I will make sure that those codes do not leave this boat.

My fingers wrap around the handle, and in quick concession, I release two bullets, one in between each of their eyes. They thought they could control and use me for their own personal gain. There was a reason that my mother fought so hard during her short life to protect me from their tight, manipulative hold. I learned from an early age that family isn't the one you are given, it is the one that you choose. I feel nothing for the lives I have just ended. I was unwillingly bound to these men, but my freedom has cost me the love of the greatest man I have ever met.

I throw my brother's phone, containing the codes onto the dock, where I am sure it will be found safely by Nixon or his staff, and tip my father's and brother's bodies overboard, watching as they sink into the black depths of the loch.

Firing up the engine, I drive out into the darkness, with one destination in mind. Hoping with all of my heart that one day the people here can find it in themselves to forgive me for my betrayal.

Thirteen

Nixon

I am found by none other than Ryan, what feels like a week later, but is in fact only the following afternoon, when the staff return to Lennox House after their Christmas night out.

Maybe I could have worked harder to free myself, but I had nothing left in me after Karina gutted me of my pride, along with my heart, spilling the evidence all over the floor of the library at my bloody and bound feet.

Watching her leave with those scumbags was devastating.

Lies and betrayal are what I have experienced in my life a hundred times over. People will use you for their own selfish cause if you let them, and I thought that I had built a fool-proof radar for bullshit. I knew she was hiding something, but I thought that it was Karina herself who was in danger, not that she *was* the danger.

If my calculations are right, the Salvadores or one of their assassins will be knocking down my gates by nightfall, and I am resigned to my fate.

I don't even lift my head when Ryan storms into the room. "Nixon, Jesus Christ, mate. Are you okay?" I know how it looks. I am still bound to the antique chair, shirtless, with my fly undone and my cock hanging out. "Holy sh- Are you okay? Should I call the doctor?"

He flies behind me, and I hear him flip open his pocketknife, the metal cold and sharp against my wrists. I don't need to look to know there are deep gashes from when I tried to free myself last night, but I barely flinch as he pushes the blade against them to slice the ties.

Ryan makes quick work of my ankles next, kneeling before me, his face green with worry. "Karina?" he asks cautiously. I can only imagine what he thinks has happened to her, with finding me in this state.

I shake my head, unable to find the words, but I know that he needs the confirmation that the unthinkable hasn't happened. "Sh-she's fine." I lick my cracked lips, the words scraping my dry throat as I force them out. "Karina Campbell is a traitorous whore, and I never want to hear her name mentioned in this house again."

Not that I will be around to see. I am about to be six feet under myself.

I guess my mate back in London was right in his concern for me and the people I chose to go into business with.

Lennox House.

I will need to call my lawyer and have the rights of the estate put into someone else's name. Maggie's perhaps. She always had my family's best interest at heart, so it seems fitting that she should be the one who decides what happens to the Lennox legacy.

I question my sudden change of heart, but I guess when everything is about to come to end, you start to think about how it all started and what will happen when you are gone. I can admit that I was wrong in my quest to tear the Lennox estate to pieces. The people here are good people. It is my father I hated, but I can't let one poisoned apple spoil the tree.

Ryan arrives on his knees before me. I hadn't even noticed that he had left. With a glass of water, he pats me on the thigh gently. "The doc is on his way. Maggie called the police when we saw the chaos outside, so they should be here any minute."

My head flies up at his words, and I ask him to elaborate.

"There are bodies everywhere down at the dock." I can't hear anymore; I need to see for myself.

Ryan helps me to my feet, and I tuck myself back into my slacks. He pulls off his hoodie and hands it to me.

I guess he's not so bad. We were both blinded by the same woman, after all. I guess there is a lesson to be learned here for both of us. I slap him on the back in a silent thank you and hobble as best as I can on my aching limbs outside. I want to get a look before the police arrive on the scene.

At first glance, I can see why Ryan was so concerned that Karina was not inside with me. It is a bloodbath out here. Two boats bob in the water, the sides all shot up and containing three dead assailants. One other body lays twisted on the dock. It looks like he tried to drag himself to safety, while one other body floats in the water face down. I push forward to get a better look when my foot kicks something.

A phone.

It is fingerprint locked, but I know what it is as soon as I see it.

It is the phone that bastard in the blue mask put my codes into.

Lifting my head, I scan the horizon, looking for her. Knowing that this is her doing.

But why?

I pocket the phone for later, knowing I can hack into it with no problem, as Ryan appears at my side. Careful not to touch anything. "What in the ever-loving hell happened here last night, Nixon?"

I consider lying to him, but he deserves the whole truth. I think it is time that Ryan and I start over. "We were attacked last night. Some shit went down in their bid to get some very lucrative information from me about one of my clients. Karina was involved with them all along."

I turn to face him, giving him a look that he will know this next part is not up for discussion. "But we will tell the police that we were attacked, they got spooked by a noise, and must have turned on one another during their escape. You found me bound this morning and called the police right away. There will be no mention of Karina Campbell's part in this, or even of her employment here."

Ryan nods, the confusion clear on his face, but I know, for some inexplicable reason, that I can trust him with this.

"Good, now go and tell Maggie the same. I will be here if there is anything else. I need some fresh air."

He leaves, just as the sirens echo in the distance.

***

6 months later.

After some digging, and with the benefit of more information on Karina's identity, it became obvious that my father knew exactly who Karina's biological father was and hoped that somehow, he would find her here and make me collateral damage in some way. It would explain why such a selfish man would allow a girl he never knew to stay in his home without giving anything in return. He didn't plot my demise himself, but he must have known I had no interest in carrying on the Earldom, so he laid me out on a silver platter for people who would. In fact, it would not surprise me if Alexander was the one who tipped off the McCloys of Karina's whereabouts.

That, ladies and gentlemen, was just the kind of bastard that my father was.

One thing that I have been able to admit to myself these past months is that I was willingly swallowing poison and expecting someone else to die.

Metaphorically speaking, of course.

I was holding on to the hatred for my father, but I was only self-harming. Denying myself of my own legacy. My own place in history. My own chance at making a difference.

The Lennox estate was not put up for sale and sold to the highest bidder. In fact, I sold my apartment in London and moved home permanently.

I ended my business amicably with all my clients. The Salvadores included. As they had no clue about the potential hack into their system, thanks to Karina. To this day, I don't know the reasons behind her actions, but I know it was her that took out her men and left the phone behind for me to find. I have spent the last few months modernising the farmland with the co-operation of the farmers and throwing myself in to the success and future of the estate to keep my mind off the redheaded vixen who landed in my life and turned it upside down.

I decided to ride Shadowfax to the Dawson farm for today's business meeting. One of the perks of living here full time now, and I am sure Shadowfax would agree. However, I still can't take a ride through the glens without thinking of Karina and day she and I rode together. That day I was so full of hope, until I wasn't. A little bit like how I feel these days with her gone completely. It is the furthest farm on our land, so I am happy that Shadowfax has gotten to stretch her legs.

One of the things I can say is that I didn't miss the unpredictable Scottish weather. There is a summer storm forecast for today, and the dark clouds are rolling in faster than predicted as we race against the clock to get back home.

We gallop over the hills, Shadowfax leaping over the streams with ease as the deer flee in the opposite direction. From us and the rain that is now coming down in sheets and bouncing off the ground.

The soil beneath her feet is quickly turning to sludge, and the first crack of thunder lights up the sky. "It's not safe for us to be out here, girl. We're going to need to find shelter."

Shadowfax protests when I pull her reins in the wrong direction. She knows I am leading her somewhere other than home and it seems she does not agree with our detour.

"Trust me," I yell over the wind and rain, my dark hair dripping into my eyes and blurring my vision. "It's too dangerous. We will find cover and wait out the storm."

Ryan's family's farm is half a mile from here. We can wait in the barn together if no one is home.

We arrive just as the thunder and lightning is in full force, the smoke from the cottage chimney telling me that someone is home. After putting Shadowfax safely in one of the stalls in the barn, I run to the house, but no one answers.

I shiver on the doorstep, water dripping off my hair, down my nose and chin.

"Hello? It's Nixon, I am just looking to ride out the storm," I call, hoping that someone answers fast before I catch hypothermia.

In a last-ditch attempt, I try the door. It's not like the Mackenzie family hasn't known me my whole life, and I hardly intend on robbing them. In fact, if I die out here, they won't have a farm to live on.

The hinges strain as I gently step out of the storm and into the Mackenzie's cozy farmhouse.

Not wanting to trail dripping water through the neat little home, I hang my drenched coat on a peg behind the door. A crack from a log burning fire sounds from the room next door.

Strange.

Why would they go out and leave the fire burning and the door unlocked?

"Hello, Mrs Mackenzie, is anyone home? I apologise for intruding in such a manner, but I was caught in the storm. I hope you don't mind my taking shelter here, while waiting for it to pass."

I am met again by nothing but the crackling of the fire. Slowly, I make my way down the hall, which opens out into an open-plan rustic kitchen and dining area, adjoined by a small sitting area.

Did they go outside to fetch something and get caught in the storm?

I pull my phone out to call Ryan, but the storm has turned my service to shit. One of the only things that I miss about London is the constant signal. A bad storm can cut you off for days up here.

Two high-back armchairs sit facing the fire, and I decide to dry out by the fire and wait for whoever has been home to return.

I stop in my tracks, blinking to clear my eyes, sure that my imagination is playing tricks on me.

Red hair spills out from the side of the armchair and tumbles over the armrest.

It cannot be. She has no reason to be here.

Swallowing the dry lump in my throat, I will my feet to keep pushing me on.

To confirm or dash my greatest of hopes.

Arriving before her, my lungs are robbed of any air left in them.

It's her.

The woman who has haunted my dreams and every waking moment since she left me.

Karina is sleeping curled up by the fire with her legs pulled to her chest.

I reach out to palm her face, when she shifts on the chair, stretching her legs to the footstool before her. She sighs in her sleep, and the first genuine smile in months pulls at my lips.

I drink her in, savouring the soft beauty of her features, and I am not sure if my eyes are just starved of her, but she looks more beautiful than ever before.

My eyes fall down her body, drinking her in when my heart sinks to my gut and I will myself to take breath deep calming breaths to keep the vomit at bay. I study her more closely, despite how painful the act is.

Sticking out through her fluffy cream jumper is a neat little baby bump. It would be almost unnoticeable if I wasn't so well acquainted with her body.

Fuck!

My legs give out from under me, and I collapse like a dead weight on to the armchair beside her. Sweat gathers at my brow, and I push my hair off my face with both hands, gripping at the roots painfully, doing everything I can to distract from the pain of my heart shredding into a thousand pieces, the blood dripping at my feet along with the rainwater.

That is why she is here and hasn't contacted me.

Karina is with Ryan now and is quite clearly having his baby.

Yet, for some inexplicable reason, I don't move an inch, still captivated by her beauty and not ready to say goodbye.

Again.

I am not ready to wake her up and have her confirm my worst fears, and irrationally, I am furious that it is not my baby she is carrying in her belly.

I sit for at least an hour, watching the beauty before me sleep and playing everything that could have been through my head. Torturing myself, knowing she belongs to someone else now.

Despite the pain and feeling like I would rather go blind than have to watch my girl carry another man's child, my eyes had not been playing a trick on me. Karina is more beautiful than ever before, because she is positively glowing. The pregnancy glow is without a doubt working its magic on my girl. My heart stings in my chest once more as I remind myself that, even in my head, I can't call her that anymore.

Karina stirs, and I brace myself for the inevitable agony, as slowly, she blinks her eyes open.

I smile at her as gently as I can, masking the hurt in my eyes like a pro from my years of practice. "Hello, little rabbit."

Karina rubs her eyes, wordlessly gazing around the room, before her blues land back on me. "Nixon." Her soft voice is a caress that my ears have been deprived of for too long.

"I see congratulations are in order." Her face twists in hurt or confusion, I cannot be sure. Which is rich from her. Out of the pair, I should be the one acting hurt here.

"I was waiting for you," she whispers, barely above the crack of the fire. "You promised that you would come for me and make me pay."

"It doesn't look like you were sitting around bored, waiting." My head nods in the direction of her blossoming stomach and the pain slices at my gut once again.

"Nixon, you have to understand-"

"I don't have to understand anything, little rabbit. After everything that happened that night, I thought I was mad at you–I *was* mad at you. However, you went ahead and took out those men, your family, and left any evidence behind for only me to find. I guess I naively thought that you would return to me once you were able."

Karina shuffles to the edge of her chair and grabs my hand, and the stupid part of me that still hopes we could ever be together, lets her, despite in my broken heart knowing that we are doomed. "Nixon, everything that happened, what I did. I wasn't sure that you ever wanted to see me again. So, I was waiting for you, as close by as I could manage, waiting for you to forgive me or hunt me down as you promised. I didn't want to cause you more pain or hurt than I already have."

I clear my throat, hoping my words come out steady so not to prompt any guilt. As Karina owes me none, I have forgiven her. I need to let her move on. "I must admit, seeing that baby growing inside of you cuts deeper than anything that has happened before now. But what is done is done, little rabbit. It is time that I let you go and wish you the best."

Tears gather at the corners of her eyes, and she quickly dashes them away, gritting her teeth. "Just like that?"

"It is for the best. Nothing good could come from keeping me in your life, Karina, you must know that."

"And what about our baby's life? After everything, you can just let us go like that. I understand that you may not be willing to give me a second chance, but you truly are the selfish son of a bitch I always thought you were if you can just turn him away like this!"

Her words tilt my entire world on its axis. "O-our baby?"

"Yes, Nixon, who else's could it be?" My eyes follow her movements as Karina drops her hand to cradle her belly as I try frantically to process what she is saying.

"I assumed it was Ryan's... Karina, you don't look like you can be any further along than four months."

Is this real life?

"Six months." Karina doesn't miss a beat while she is staring at me like I have two heads.

"Th-that is *our* baby you are growing in there?"

She nods while looking down and cradling the tiny bump.

My head flies from her belly to her face when I replay her words in my head.

"You said turn *him* away. You know it's a boy?" Am I awake right now, or is this another one of my cruel dreams?

"Yes, I might not be showing much, but he is a big, strong, healthy boy. I swear he is doing chin-ups in my belly at night when I am trying to sleep."

I barely give her a chance to finish before I am lifting her and dragging her onto my lap. I capture her delighted squeal with my mouth and devour her like the starving man I am. It doesn't take long before Karina is moaning into my mouth and sucking on my tongue and lips.

It seems that my girl is just as hungry as me.

I tear my mouth away from hers and pull her sweater over her head, her belly on proud display right before me, making my cock twitch beneath her.

I tug the cups of her bra under her swollen breasts, covering one with my mouth and rolling the other between my knuckles, until her nipples are rock solid and she is grinding on me like a seasoned stripper.

"Does that feel good, baby?"

Karina nods and pulls my head further onto her breast. "Yes! They have been so sensitive; I swear, I get aroused from the slightest graze."

I groan my approval. "And what about this pretty little pussy? Has she missed me too?"

"Yes," she pants a breathless whisper in the small space between us.

I pull her panties tightly against her folds. "Have you let anyone else touch my pussy since I planted that baby deep inside of you?"

Karina continues grinding on me over my trousers, and I wait with bated breath for her answer. The thought of anyone else touching Karina makes me frenzied, never mind when she is growing our baby inside of her.

"Don't make me ask again, little rabbit." I pull on her nipples hard before soothing them with my mouth and tongue.

"Ah, Nixon!" she moans and swivels her hips, desperately trying to find friction against something.

I spank her full arse, relishing in the way it ripples before gripping her hips with both hands. "Not an answer." I pull my cock out and line it up with her entrance, but not giving her what we are both desperate for before she gives me my answer.

"No, never! You have ruined me for anyone else. Just like you promised you would. But I wouldn't go back and change a thing. I wouldn't have it any other way."

I slide her down my length, and we moan and pant into one another. "I am yours, and you are mine. Say it for me, baby."

"I am yours, and you are mine," she chants through her whimpers. "Every inch of your beautifully broken black heart belongs to me, Nixon Lennox, and don't you ever forget it."

With her words, she secures her hold around my neck and fucks me with everything that she's got, bouncing and rocking on my lap like a temptress. Taking every inch of me like it is her God-given right. I watch as I disappear inside of her over and over as she coats my length with her arousal.

I sit back and admire the goddess before me, round and swollen with the evidence of my seed, and the possessive asshole in me has never seen a more breathtaking sight. I would put another baby inside of her right now if I could. That is when I decide that I am going to put as many kids inside of Karina as she will let me.

I roll my thumb over her slippery clit and tell her how I plan on keeping her pregnant so that everyone will see that she belongs to me irrevocably. I suck on her hard little nipples as I promise that we will fill Lennox House with children who are happy and loved, and she shatters around me, coming all over my cock when I tell her that I will be making her my wife, and I will love her until the day that I die.

***

"Why Ryan?"

The storm has passed, and we are sitting curled up in front of the fire. I will need to ask for Thomas to drive down with the land rover and ride Shadowfax back to Lennox House. I can't have Karina on the back in her current condition.

Karina drags her fingertips over my forearms repeatedly, leaving goosebumps in her wake and I stop myself from purring like a damn kitten under her undivided attention.

"Despite what you always thought, I knew I could trust him. I made sure to lay low for a few days. Waited for the police to be done with their investigation on the estate, and then I made my way to the Mackenzie house, to beg Ryan and his family for shelter. I made them promise not to say a word, that I wanted you to find me on your own. Then I found out that I was pregnant, and things got messy in my head. I didn't want to wait you out. I wanted you. No, I needed you. But I was too scared of how you would react to seeing me again and I had our baby to think about. It wasn't just me anymore. I didn't know if you would be delighted or horrified when you found out.

I tighten my arms around her waist, squeezing her gently. Punching my own face repeatedly in my head at not tracking her down myself. My stomach churns at the thought of not finding her tonight. What if I hadn't of stopped at the Mackenzie house? I would never have found her.

"Don't think like that," my girl reassures, reading my mind. "Everything happens for a reason; things have worked out exactly how they were supposed to. Don't beat yourself up. We both must shoulder some blame. In fact, I would say that I am responsible for most of the heartbreak caused here."

"You killed your family for me." It is not a question.

Karina stares into the fire for a moment, the memories of that night clearly flashing through her mind as they also do mine, often. "They weren't my family. My father has done nothing but use me from the moment he came into my life. It wouldn't have stopped with you; he would have found another way to use and manipulate me. It haunts me still, but I know I did the right thing, especially after finding out I was pregnant."

My fists flex, thinking about my unborn son in the hands of those monsters, and I have never been so grateful and proud of the brave and courageous woman in my arms.

"I will never let anything happen to you ever again. I love that you fought for me, and I will spend the rest of my life fighting for you and that little guy that you have been keeping safe inside of you. You will be a wonderful mother, Karina, and I promise to protect our family with the same fervency that you do. Be my wife, Karina, and I promise I will fight for the family that we will grow together, so that you never have to fight alone again."

EPILOGUE

Karina

3 months later

"This can't be happening!" I bend over the bed, bracing my weight with one hand while the other cradles my stomach.

Maggie is at my back, rubbing firm, hard circles over the base of my spine. "I'm afraid it is, my dear. You have to be brave; this baby is on his way, whether you are ready for him or not."

I fall to my knees and fist the bedsheets like they have wronged me in another life, and how I wish they were Nixon's neck right now for putting me through this pain without him. My water broke when I got out of the bath and my contractions have been coming thick and fast ever since.

"I thought labour with your first was supposed to be slow," I cry into Maggie's shoulder as she wipes the matted hair from my face. "Where the hell is Nixon? I thought that you called him."

I didn't plan on having a home birth, but it looks like our son will be as impatient as his father. There is no way we will make it to the hospital in time, and I refuse to give birth on the side of a highland road, in a failed attempt to make it to the delivery ward.

Goddamnit, where is my husband?

"He can't miss this, Maggie." I am cold and shivering and pain like I have never felt before has overtaken my entire body.

"I know, child. He is on his way. Try to conserve your energy," she soothes in a motherly way, and terror seizes me at the thought of not being able to be the mother our son deserves. What if it doesn't come naturally like everyone always tells you it will?

Nixon, where are you, goddamnit?

"I need him!" I plead like a child as our cook lays towels on our bed and helps me to my feet.

"He will be here," she repeats, and I don't know if she is trying to convince me or herself. "We need you in bed, dear. Let me take another look."

Maggie has managed to set up the iPad and is on a video call with one of the midwives from the hospital, who is assuring us that my obstetrician is already on her way.

I lie on the bed, groaning in pain, this new position so much worse than before.

"Hold me in front of Karina, Maggie." She does as she is told, and I open my legs, not caring at this point if there is a livestream being broadcast around the globe. All of my dignity has flown out of the window. I don't care about anything but getting this baby out and this pain being over. "Okay, he is crowning, Karina. On your next contraction, I am going to need you to take a deep breath and push for me."

Panic floods me, and I try to get off the bed, before Maggie gently presses me back against the headboard. "He will be here," she tells me, this time with fire in her eyes. Telling me without words that we can do this.

"I can't do this without Nixon." More tears roll down my soaked face as the reality of having to do just that sets in.

The words barely leave my mouth before a contraction builds stronger than any other. I grip the pillows, desperately wishing that it was Nixon's hand I was clutching. I scream through the pain and push while Maggie counts aloud to five.

"You are doing it, darling!" she shouts from between my legs.

I am about to disagree with her, when the bedroom door flies open, and Nixon strides in, like a bat out of hell. His raven hair in disarray and eyes wild as they search for me. His face pales even further than his already fair complexion as he takes in the scene before him. Without another word, he strides in my direction, cupping my face and pulling me in for a kiss the moment that he reaches me.

"I'm so sorry, little rabbit. I turned the car around as soon as I got the call. I'm sure I broke every speeding law to get back to you. How are you feeling, baby?"

My answer comes with another scream as I push through the next contraction. Nixon grabs my hand and wraps his arm around my back.

"Is she supposed to be in this much pain?" Nixon directs his question towards the midwife on the screen, his voice full of fear and concern.

"That's his little head out, dear," Maggie shouts, reminding us of her presence.

"You've got this, baby. Look, you've done all the hard work without me. My little warrior." Nixon smirks in that devastating way I adore, and I can't help but laugh through the pain.

"As far as I see it, you only participated in the fun part." Nixon arches his brow knowingly and dips his mouth to mine in a gentle caress.

Another guest enters, led by one of the maids, and relief washes through the room.

"I'm here, I'm here. Sorry that it took so long," Doctor Mulholland announces as she slides on a pair of gloves and settles between my legs. "One more push, Mrs Lennox, and he will be here."

The pressure mounts once again, and with one final push, our beautiful baby is born. Maggie pulls my nightgown aside as Doctor Mulholland places our screaming son on my bare chest.

Nixon crouches at my side, tears gathering in the corners of his eyes, and places his head against mine as we take in our son. "Well done, baby. I am so bloody proud of you. I never doubted you for a minute."

"Does he have a name?" Dr Mulholland asks as she busies herself between my legs, but I can't feel anything anymore, only the overwhelming joy of finally holding our son in my arms.

"Nova." I smooth his dark tuft of hair, and smile softly at his furrowed brow and adorably obnoxious pout, already seeing that he is going to take after his father.

Nixon places a hand over his tiny back, almost covering it completely with one palm, and Nova immediately settles. My heart feels like it is about to explode with the amount of love it is trying to contain. I know Nixon will be everything that his father never was. "Welcome to the world, Nova Lennox. The 17th Earl of Lennoxshire. You and I are going to have some adventures together. I can't wait to teach you everything that I know. This right here is your momma; she is the queen of our house, and she saved our family in more ways than I can ever say. Maybe one day, we will sit down over a pint, and I will fill you in on it all."

"Well, maybe not everything," I warn him with a gentle smile.

Nixon slides his hand into my hair and pulls me towards his lips, a knowing smirk playing at the side of his mouth. "No, little rabbit, some parts of you will always be kept just for me."

THE END

Thank you!

If you have made it this far, thank you so much for taking a chance on this small-time indie author.
If you enjoyed Karina & Nixon's story, it would mean the world to me if you could please leave a small review on any platform. Your support means more that you know.
Nixon is a story that I have always wanted to write but never thought people were interested in reading.
However, these characters have been niggling away at me for so long, that I decided to put my third book in the Twisted Alliance Series on hold and really write something for me. The whole process has been so cathartic for me, during a time of chaos in my personal life and I hope that at least one person can enjoy reading it as much as I enjoyed writing it.
Much love,
Jane
x

Also by Jane Ace

Stand Alone
Young, Rich & Sinful
(Available only in paperback)

Twisted Alliance Series
Vows of Violence
Acts of Violence
Fear of Violence (Coming soon)

Printed in Great Britain
by Amazon

37397246R00096